A LOVE TO CONQUER

MAIL ORDER BRIDE ROMANCE

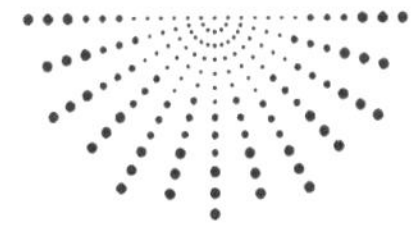

INDIANA WAKE

CHAPTER ONE

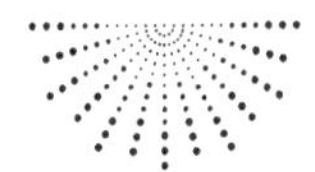

There was not a cloud in the sky, and the air was dewy. The night sky was covered with a carpet of stars, the full moon was out in all of its grandeur and the street was quiet... and still.

Ada Wright sat by the window, gazing at the stars. Her long, reddish-brown hair billowed in the breeze as she let her mind drift to the events of the ending day. It was one of those difficult days where worry clouded her mind and weighed her down. Ada missed the early years when she first started working as a caregiver and cook for Jane Gilbert. When times were simpler and Jane was much stronger. But all that had changed. Now all Ada did was worry over Jane's health.

"I still can't fall asleep," Ada heard Jane say from the bed. "I'm not tired."

Ada turned around and smiled at Jane. "Is my presence helping, or not?"

"It is," Jane answered weakly.

"Are you sure about that? Because I think it'll be much better if I return to my room and leave you alone. I think I'm distracting you."

"You're not," Jane said. "I don't want to be alone tonight. Just wait for a bit, the medicine will soon kick in. I know how much you love sky gazing, so continue doing that. You can leave when I fall asleep, please, I don't want to be alone."

"Of course," Ada answered. "Do you need me to get you anything? Some warm milk might help."

Jane coughed and shook her head. "I'm fine. I'm too weak to sit up anyway."

Ada rose from her seat and walked over to the bed. She sat by Jane's side and took her hand. "Does your chest still hurt?"

"It doesn't hurt that much," Jane answered.

"Do you still feel cold? Do you need me to get you more blankets? I can feel you shivering underneath the covers."

"I'm fine," Jane said again, chuckling. "Don't get agitated, Ada. If I need anything, I'll let you know. For a young woman like yourself, you tend to worry like a grandmother."

"I'm right to worry," Ada said. "You're sick, and you need to get better soon so we can knit sweaters together. It'll soon be winter, and you promised me that we'll be making new sweaters before the summer is over."

"Oh, winter is months away. We still have time."

Ada let out a sigh and dropped her head. Jane had been sick for over a year now, and there were no positive signs that she was getting any better. There were many more visible strands of grey hair on her head that weren't there a few months ago. Wrinkles had now taken over her once smooth face. It took Ada too long to realize that her dear employer and friend was getting old.

Ada had sent for multiple doctors and nurses to examine Jane, but they couldn't give a definite cause for Jane's ailment. It was either the common cold, a stomach infection, a mere headache...or the likes. Jane had gone through so many treatments, and yet it didn't look like she was getting any better; in fact, it felt like she was getting worse.

Jane was the only family that Ada had. They were not related by blood, but they had a bond as a mother had with her daughter. Ada had looked after Jane for five years. She recalled her first day vividly. Ada had just turned twenty, and she had heard that Jane was looking for a housekeeper. From the very first day that she spoke to Jane, she took to her and the feeling was reciprocated. They had lived harmoniously together all those years. Ada couldn't imagine her life anywhere else.

"You know I adore you?" Jane said weakly. "You are the daughter I never had. You're beautiful with fierce blue eyes that can melt any heart, and you're caring, kind, and selfless. I don't know what I would have done without you."

Ada blinked back the tears that were threatening to fall. "Thank you." She giggled and sniffed. "You know I don't do well with compliments, Jane. You're going to make me cry."

Jane squeezed Ada's hand. "Before I pass away, I'll make sure to include you in my will, Ada. You deserve it more than anyone else. I've been sick for so long, but you have been the only person that stuck by my side. That says a lot considering I have a son too who didn't think to visit. I'll make sure to leave you the better part of my estate. Especially, this house. I will rest well knowing that they are in your care."

Ada wiped the tear that had fallen on her cheek. "You're speaking as if you're dying anytime soon, Jane. You have many good years of life left."

It wasn't the first time Jane had hinted that she was going to include Ada in her will and leave most of her estate in her name. Given that her son lived far away and never thought to visit, even after Jane wrote him so many letters, Ada could understand why Jane wanted her to inherit her properties. They trusted and loved each other that much. But Ada didn't care for all of that. She was more interested in spending time with Jane and keeping her alive as long as she could.

"Hopefully," Jane said with a faint smile. "Do you have any future plans, Ada? What do you want to do? You're young, and you have your whole life ahead of you."

Ada hadn't really given her future much thought. She was comfortable working with Jane and imagined living with her for as long as she could. Finding good places to work was difficult in Virginia, and Ada was thankful that she got a job she loved. As for future plans, well... she hadn't thought that far.

"I can't think of anything yet," she answered. "Frankly, I like this job. I like living with you, taking care of you. If there's ever a need to plan another path for myself, then I will do so then."

"Do what makes you happy, all right?" Jane said. "That's what's important. During my youth, I didn't do much. I have very few fond memories that I hold on to and reminisce about. Most of them are the times I spent with you. It's not a lot. I want you to create lasting memories. You'll have this house to yourself, and a couple of other properties. Make the best of the time you have. Trust me, it goes by in a flash."

"I have all the time in the world to figure it out, Jane. There's no rush. What I want right now, is for you to get well soon, so we can make those blankets and sweaters before summer is over. Tomorrow, I'll go to the market and buy the wool for us to use. I noticed you're stronger in the mornings, so we can knit for a bit before you have to lay down again. Is that a good idea?"

"It is," Jane said, coughing. She reached for her napkin, folded on the table, and covered her mouth with it.

Ada inched closer to her and placed a hand on Jane's chest. She gently tapped on it as the doctor had shown her. Jane hacked on for more than a minute. The doctor had said worrying wasn't going to do Jane any good, so it was best that Ada didn't show her fear. But whenever Ada heard Jane's uncontrollable coughing, she panicked and her heart raced.

"Oh, that can't be good," Jane said, staring at the napkin.

Ada swiftly rose from the bed and took the napkin from Jane. She inhaled nervously at the sight of blood. Jane had never coughed up blood before.

"Why isn't the medicine doing any good?" Ada whispered in a quivering voice and touched her palm to her head. "You should be getting better, not hacking up blood."

"I'm tired," Jane said, nearly out of breath.

"I'll get you some water, and I'll send for the doctor right away."

"It's too late at night to fetch the doctor."

"He'll come," Ada insisted. "Let me get you some water first."

Ada scurried out of the room and into the kitchen. The doctor had told Ada the last time he came that he couldn't say for certain if the medicine would have any effect on Jane's health. Regardless of that, Ada wanted to be optimistic. But her hope was slowly dwindling.

With the cup of water in hand, Ada returned to the room. "Jane, let me help you sit up," she said, setting the cup down on the bedside table.

Jane's eyes were shut, and she seemed to have fallen asleep. A part of Ada wanted to leave her to sleep peacefully, but it was strange. She had only been gone for a moment.

"Jane?" Ada called softly. She reached for Jane's shoulder and shook it.

The sound of her palpitating heart was distracting Ada from focusing. She was starting to panic. Jane was still. Too still.

"Jane! What's wrong?"

Deep down, Ada knew it had happened, but she didn't want to believe it. She was not going to accept it.

Vigorously, Ada shook Jane's body as tears rolled down her eyes. "I'll go fetch the doctor. Jane, open your eyes. Wake up!"

It couldn't be. She was talking just minutes ago. Ada staggered off the bed and ran out of the room. Her vision was blurry, but she kept running and praying that Jane wasn't gone. That it was all a dream.

CHAPTER TWO

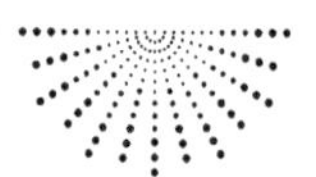

wo weeks later...

Jane was actually gone.

It all still felt surreal. Ada had seen the lifeless body of her friend on that bed. The doctor had pronounced Jane dead, and a few days after that, Jane was six feet under the ground. Still, it didn't feel real. Ada still held on to the hope that it was all a dream. But dreams didn't last so long.

Ada touched her forehead and sighed. Lately, it was difficult to get up every morning. Her eyes were puffy, and her head hurt too much. A feeling of numbness had also taken over her body. Nothing felt real anymore.

"You're going to hurt yourself if you keep crying, Ada," Mary said to her.

She was seated at the edge of the bed with sulking lips. Her dark brown hair was disheveled and there were dark circles under her eyes. She too had stayed awake all night with Ada.

Mary Radford was Ada's only friend in the town. They met the first day Ada moved into the neighborhood and had been good friends ever since. Apart from Jane, Mary was the only person that truly knew Ada. They were like sisters. Mary always looked out for Ada, and Ada did the same.

"What am I going to do, Mary?" Ada asked in a weak tone. "I can't believe Jane is gone. One moment she was here, and the next she was no more."

"That's how life is," Mary said with a sigh. She ran her fingers through her hair and shook her head. "So unpredictable. Things happen in a flash, and we have no control over the outcome of certain events. I would have never believed Jane passed away if I didn't see her myself. I still can't believe it. I won't ever see her smile again, or listen to her witty jokes. We can only hope she's in a better place."

Paul Gilbert, Jane's only son, was in town. He had arrived a week after Jane's death. He had helped out during Jane's burial, but he and Ada had barely said more than ten words to each other. He arrived with his wife, Clara Gilbert. They had never spoken, but Ada always caught her condescending stares. They were not a friendly bunch, but it didn't bother Ada since she was always inside her room.

"Does Mrs. Jane's son know that Jane left you this house?"

Ada glanced at Mary and sighed. She had barely given the issue of Jane's properties any thought since her death. But with Paul around, and given their cold demeanor, Ada knew she had to discuss it eventually.

"I'm not prepared to handle that now, Mary. When it's time, we'll know what to do."

Just then, a hard, loud knock on her door garnered both their attention. Ada jerked and sat up from the bed with a puzzled look on her face.

"Who in the world could that be?" Ada asked.

"I'll check."

Mary hurriedly made her way to the door. Paul and Clara usually didn't come to her room for anything, hence, it baffled Ada that one of them was knocking so rudely on her door.

Mary opened the door to reveal Paul standing in front of it. "We need to talk. Come to the living room," was all he said before walking away.

Ada and Mary exchanged puzzled looks. "I wonder what the problem is," Ada said, pushing the covers aside.

"What do you think?" Mary asked.

Once Ada was dressed they both walked to the living room and found Paul and Clara standing side by side, arms crossed. Paul was a lanky man, with perpetually rough, brown hair and weathered skin. Clara, on the other hand, was plump and had short and puffy curly hair.

"So, we've been hearing news around town that you're trying to steal my mother's properties."

Ada's jaw instinctively dropped, clearly taken aback by the man's words. "I'm sorry?"

"Steal?" Mary asked. "Jane left this house for Ada and a part of her estate too."

Paul and Clara scoffed simultaneously. "Why would my mother leave her properties to you?"

"I'm not trying to steal anything. Before Jane passed away, she talked about giving this house to me because she has a lot of things here that are dear to her heart and she wanted me to take proper care of them."

"That's not your concern," Paul said. "My mother's only will is in my possession and there is no mention of you anywhere in it. She was merely thinking of leaving you something, but she never did. I understand that you might be desperate to hold on to something, but don't be greedy."

"I don't want to discuss this now, I miss Jane, and all I want is the chance to grieve her," Ada said with a quivering voice.

"Then you can continue doing so. As far as I'm concerned, your services in this house are no longer needed. You were employed as a housekeeper and a cook. Your job here is done. I don't see any reason why you're still here."

"You shouldn't speak to Ada like this," Mary chimed in. "She and Jane were very close and it's expected that Jane's death hit her pretty hard. It's harsh of you to chase her away. We all know that Mrs. Jane wanted Ada to have this house. You can ask my employer, Mr. Peyton from the next house where I work. He knows it too."

"So, you want to fight this? When we clearly have my mother's will?" Paul asked.

Mary sighed. "No one is..."

"Mary," Ada said, cutting her off. "I don't want to argue. It hasn't been long since we buried Jane. The last thing I want to do is sour her memory with an ugly conflict."

"Ada, you can't let them take this house from you," Mary whispered.

Ada scanned the living room where she had shared so many memories with Jane and sighed. Mary was right to ask her to fight it, but Ada didn't want Jane rolling in her grave. Jane had left. Perhaps it was time for her to leave too. Perhaps, it was time to start a new life somewhere else.

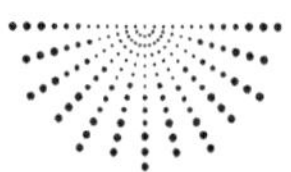

CHAPTER THREE

In a small town in Minnesota called Fairview, Flynn Holt stood outside his recently established boarding house with his hands on his hips and a proud smile on his face. It had easily become a routine for him. Although the boarding house had been in operation for a few months now, Flynn always stood here, to admire it every morning. It gave him pleasure to look at the results of his hard work and persistence.

"Maybe if you stare at it for long enough, it'll turn to gold."

Flynn turned to find his friend, Kit shaking his head at him. At Kit's side was Pearl, his wife. Pearl had one hand on her hip and her head was tilted to the left as if she was trying to change the perspective of the building. They had watched him carry out this routine every morning, so it was only typical that they were starting to make fun of him.

"I'll stop." Flynn chuckled. "No, maybe I won't. It does a man good to admire his hard work." He brushed his short blond hair back with his fingers and placed his hat on his head.

"Hard work." Kit blew out some air and then grinned. His vibrant red hair was sticking out from beneath his hat and his face was a little more wrinkled than Flynn's. The man was tall and wiry, and when he smiled, which he did often, there was one tooth missing in the front making him look a little comical.

"Where are you both coming from so early in the morning? "Flynn asked.

"We went for a walk," Kit answered, taking his wife's hand. "It's a nice day for a walk."

"It's hot," Flynn answered. "It's a hot day and you went for a walk?"

Flynn always wondered how Kit and Pearl never got tired of each other. Kit was Flynn's good friend. Before Pearl arrived, they were always together. All the while,

Flynn never imagined Kit with a woman. The man always claimed love was an exaggeration, and he wasn't looking forward to being saddled with a wife. But then, one day, he decided to put out an advert for a mail-order-bride, and a few months later, Pearl showed up in Minnesota. Since then, Kit had become a completely different man. Love had changed him for the better.

Kit had tried to convince Flynn to put in his own advert for a mail-order bride, but Flynn declined. He did not like to wear his heart on his sleeve. The one thing he feared the most was getting his heart broken. Hence, he never gave it to anyone. The idea of waiting for days, weeks, or months for a reply from someone across the country was nerve-wracking. Could you believe what they said? There was a lot that could go wrong with something like that.

Kit and Pearl were always by Flynn's side. They were his biggest supporters and they all ran the boarding house together. The two of them were the only people Flynn could count on for anything. They sacrificed their time and resources for him and never complained. They were excited about his ideas too and were even more excited to be a part of them.

"How's the search for a cook going?"

Flynn let out a sigh. He walked over to their side and leaned on the wall. "I can't seem to find anyone. It's as if no one in this town is interested."

Flynn had not only established a boarding house, but he had also turned an empty hall beside it into a restaurant. At first, the plan sounded brilliant. The restaurant was supposed to lure more people that were traveling into the boarding house. There were a few eateries around the town, but he wanted one of his own. One close to the railway tracks. Sadly, finding a cook was proving to be difficult. It was taking months.

"Maybe we should ask around," Kit suggested. "Perhaps word hasn't gotten out far enough."

"It has," Flynn answered. "I don't know what the issue is. I'm starting to think the idea was terrible, after all. Perhaps I should have just stuck with the boarding house and nothing else."

"I have a suggestion," Pearl said, glancing at the both of them. "A good one. A tested one, and a trusted one."

Flynn threw both hands in the air. "Please, I'm all ears."

Pearl turned to Kit and gave him a bright smile. "You know the story of how I met Kit, Flynn. It wasn't an accident or coincidence. I saw his advert in the paper for a bride, and it piqued my interest. I decided to come here to Minnesota, all the way from Maine of my own free will to marry him because I was sure he was the one. I assure you, Flynn, that a well-written letter can change everything and connect you to the person you need. No one would travel far if they weren't sure that they'd be a good fit. How about you write up an advert and pop it in the paper?"

"I agree with Pearl on this, Flynn. Frankly, when I sat down to write that advert for the newspaper, I was nervous. But I decided to be myself and just wrote out what was true and important. Look at me now. I met my soulmate."

Flynn paused to think. "Writing an advert might take a while. Who knows when it would pique someone's interest? If I find the right person, would they be willing to move as fast as I need?"

"That's not your problem," Kit told him. "All you have to do is put it in the paper. Leave the rest to whoever picks up the newspaper and reads the advert."

"I assure you, Flynn. Someone will write back. Not just anyone. Someone who fits the role. It worked out for Kit and me, didn't it?"

Kit and Pearl giggled at each other and shared a gentle kiss.

Flynn nodded as he allowed their suggestion to seep into his mind. Writing an advert was actually a good idea. He had been searching for a cook within the town to no avail. Perhaps it was time to broaden the search. Kit loved the idea of hiring someone who knew what they wanted, rather than someone in the town who would apply merely because there was an opening.

Owning and running a boarding house and a restaurant had been his dream for the longest time. It was a passion of his, and to see it materialize was the breath of fresh air that he needed. It would be great if the cook shared his passion and vision for his business. Flynn needed someone strong-willed and kindhearted. Someone who wouldn't take his business for granted, and someone he could count on.

"So, will you do it?" Pearl asked. "All you have to do is write the advert, and I'll take it to the paper for you. Trust me on this, Flynn. It might take time, and it might not, but it will work."

"I'll do it," Flynn announced. "I have nothing to lose and the idea intrigues me. I'll write the advert today and we'll send it. Hopefully, it'll find us the right person for the job."

"Great," Pearl said excitedly.

They talked for a while before retreating into the boarding house to start the day. There were a lot of other things that Flynn had not yet put in place, so he spent the rest of the day doing it.

The new chairs for the restaurant had just arrived from the carpenter some days ago, and they were scattered all over the place. Flynn spent the day putting everything in order before going to examine the rooms in the boarding house at night. He had promised Kit that he was going to stop gazing at his building first thing in the morning, but a part of Flynn knew he was still going to continue the routine.

Maybe, someday soon, he would be able to gaze at his restaurant too. How he hoped this idea would work for he couldn't manage much longer without extra help.

CHAPTER FOUR

"**A**re you really just going to allow them to have their way? To steal this from you?"

Ada set the newspaper down and turned to stare out of the window at the night sky. Strangely, stargazing didn't excite her like it used to. Also, she didn't like knitting anymore, and she'd rather sit at home all day and wait for the night to fall. It was not the best way to live, but she couldn't think of anything she wanted to do with herself.

After her encounter with Paul, Ada left the house that night. Mr. Peyton, Mary's employer, was kind enough to allow her to stay with Mary for the time being, at least until she sorted everything out and discovered what to do.

About two days after the encounter with Paul, Ada had heard that Paul and Clara had plans to rent out the place and return to their home in Ohio. It devastated Mary to think that Paul Gilbert had no regard for his mother's memory.

If only he had taken the time to visit her and talk to Jane, then perhaps Jane would have passed on with no worries at all in the world. But he hadn't thought it important and didn't even send a single letter all the time his mother was ill.

There were days when Jane missed her son and worried for him. Those were the days they sat down to write the letters they sent to him. When Jane's health took a turn for the worse, Ada wrote to him again, asking him to come and pay her a visit. But Paul didn't even send a letter back. It was sickening to think that he held his mother in such little regard.

Clara herself had only met with Jane a few times before Jane passed away. The last time Jane saw her was at the wedding and after that, she heard nothing from her daughter-in-law. Jane never really liked Clara. According to her, she could never tell what Clara was thinking. But since Paul wanted to marry her, Jane wanted to get to like the woman, but she never managed to do so.

"Ada?" Mary called out to her. "Are you listening to me?"

Ada snapped back to reality. "I'm sorry. I was deep in thought."

"Clearly," Mary said. "Are you really not going to fight this? Even for Jane's sake? You know how much she loved that house. It makes no sense for a complete stranger to live there."

"It really makes no sense, if we're honest." Ada sighed. "But Paul is her son. I was merely a worker there. No matter how close Jane and I were, he still remains her only living relative. We're not tied by blood and with no will... I have no say in the matter."

"Yes, you do. Everyone in the street thinks so too," Mary insisted. "Where were they when Jane was sick and wanted her son by her side? You've been working here for five years. Paul barely visited. He has a life in Ohio and a business too. Does it make sense that he won't let you have what Jane wanted you to have?"

"I'm not trying to make excuses for him, but I'm sure he prioritized his work over spending time with his mother.

That's the mistake we all make. We think what is ours will be ours forever. But that's not always the case. We don't value what we have until we lose it. Paul probably thought he had all the time in the world to spare. But you're right. If Jane wanted me to have her house, it would be unfair if I sit around and let a random stranger live there, especially as Paul intends to rent it out."

"My point exactly," Mary said. "Fight this."

"I don't want to fight, Mary," Ada said. "How would Jane feel if she sees me fighting with her son? I can't soil her memory that way. She doesn't deserve it. The best I can do is get Paul to reason with me or find another way to get to him. But he wants to fight me because he has Jane's only written will, and I can't give him that satisfaction."

"So, what are you going to do now?" Mary asked.

"I don't know, Mary," Ada answered, almost in a whisper. "But my life here in Virginia is already over. Everything reminds me of Jane and it saddens me. I've been mourning her for weeks and it still feels as though there's a weight on my chest. There's nothing left for me here. I have nowhere to stay, no job. Nothing."

"You have me."

"I know, I'm sorry, but I don't have a future and I can't live with you forever."

Mary remained silent. She dropped her head as if only just realizing the bitter truth. Ada lifted the newspaper in her hand and continued reading through it. Perhaps it was because she was thinking about a new job, but as she skimmed through the paper, an advert caught her attention. She stopped to read it when she spotted the word 'cook'.

"Fairview, Minnesota...

It was perfect. Far from Virginia and something she could do well enough since she knew her way around the kitchen.

"Look at this, Mary," Ada said, handing her the paper. "It says they are looking for a cook at a restaurant in Minnesota. I could write back?"

Mary took her time to read through the advertisement. "You're perfect for this, but Minnesota? Are you really planning on leaving Virginia?"

"Mary, all my prospects are all but dead in the water. I think I should apply for this position before someone else does."

"Ada..."

"You understand my point, Mary, you're just choosing not to agree with me. I need to find my own life. I need to grieve and let go of the things that remind me of what has happened. I have grown bitter because everything reminds me of Jane. Funnily enough, Jane and I talked about it right before she died. It was almost as if she knew. She asked me what my plan was for the future and what I liked to do. She told me to do what makes me happy. Cooking makes me happy and I have to do something for myself. I'm writing back to this man."

"Is cooking really what you want to do, or is it the only thing you can do?" Mary asked. "Does it really make you happy, or are you just saying that because you don't know how to do anything else better?"

"I really like to cook, Mary. Jane knew it too. I love to knit too, but I've only done it with Jane. She taught me how to make sweaters thick enough for winter. It always made me happy to knit with her. I could never do it alone. Cooking, on the other hand, is something I can do alone. I love to cook."

Mary gave Ada a weak smile and nodded. "I'll get you some writing materials."

The idea of a fresh start sent an exhilarating feeling down Ada's spine. It was the first time since Jane's death that something had piqued her interest that much.

A new life in another town didn't sound like a bad idea. Perhaps it was what she needed to get back on her feet. She needed to plan her move to Minnesota as soon as possible. But first, she needed to write a letter, stating her interest in working at that restaurant.

All Ada hoped was that the new start wouldn't turn out to be a nightmare. A month ago, she had been living happily with Jane, talking about knitting sweaters, replacing the floorboard in Jane's room, and just enjoying her life.

All that had changed in the blink of an eye. A plan for her future was much needed. Now more than ever. She needed to leave Virginia behind.

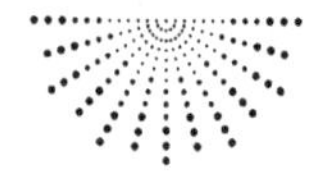

CHAPTER FIVE

Six weeks later...

"No tears. You promised, Mary."

Letters had been exchanged, tickets sent and Ada... was set to travel. She had exchanged letters with one Flynn Holt, the owner of the restaurant and he had promised to meet her at the train platform in Minnesota when her train arrived.

The time Ada spent packing her bags had been difficult. It saddened her to think that she was leaving all her memories in Virginia behind and going to start a new life somewhere she had only heard about. She would know no one... but there was only Mary to keep her here and that was not enough. As well as the fear, it was exciting to know that there was another world waiting for her, far away from her painful memories.

The day before, Ada had visited Jane's grave to say good-bye. For a brief moment, she hesitated. Even though she wasn't going to see Jane physically anymore, it was hard going so far away. Ada comforted herself with the fact that Jane's presence would be with her wherever she went. She told herself that there was nothing to be depressed about. She was going to hold on to the happy memories she had of Jane and take life one day at a time.

One regret Ada had, as she stood there on the platform ready to board the train, was that she was too weak to grant Jane's last wish. She had no voice in the situation, and Paul had the upper hand, but Ada felt guilty leaving the house to Paul. It was never about the property, ownership, or money for her. It was about preserving Jane's possessions. The beloved mirror in her room that she claimed her grandmother passed down to her; letters from Jane's father to her mother that they had exchanged during the war; Jane's favorite teacup that she had owned since she was five years old, all of those things were going to be boxed away somewhere or thrown out like they meant nothing.

Still, Ada managed to get the teacup from the house before leaving. She had also taken knitted sweaters from the house that she and Jane had made last year. Jane's memory was alive in her heart, and she planned to keep it that way.

"I'm not crying," Mary sniffed. "There's just something in my eye."

Ada giggled and hugged her for the third time since they got to the railway platform. "Right. We'll meet again. This isn't goodbye."

"Are you sure about that?" Mary sniffed.

Ada shook her head. "No, I won't say I'm sure. But I'll write to you, every chance I get. When I get to Minnesota and hopefully, once I settle in, I'll send a letter to you telling you all about the trip. Trust me."

Mary nodded and wiped the tears that had fallen on her cheeks. "I'll be expecting your letter. If anything goes wrong, come back, all right? We'll start all over again. Don't try to force anything. If, in the end, this man in Minnesota doesn't employ you, come back to Virginia. I can talk to Mr. Peyton. He can help you find a place to work here in Virginia."

"Mr. Peyton has already done too much for me, Mary," Ada said. "It'll be selfish of me to ask him to do any more. Don't worry. I'm staying optimistic. I'll do well and I'm positive Mr. Holt will employ me. I'll write to you, don't worry."

Mary nodded reluctantly. "Take very good care of yourself, all right? Eat well too and don't work too hard. I'll keep looking for ways that you can win this fight with Jane's son, Paul."

Ada shook her head. "Mary, you don't have to. No good will come out of it. Let's just accept it."

"Don't worry about it. Just go to Minnesota and settle into your new life. I know it might be a fruitless fight, but I still feel like I need to do something. It doesn't sit right with me. I'll fight in your stead. I live next to the house, so it's not like I'm going out of my way. Just go and get that job."

Mary was never one to quit. No good was going to come from fighting Paul for possession of the house, but if Mary was determined on doing it, Ada couldn't stop her. She was going to be far away from the town soon, starting a new life in a new town anyway.

"I'll miss you, Mary," Ada said with a faint smile. "Take care."

Mary wrapped her hands around Ada's neck and squeezed. "I'll miss you too. Bye, Ada. See you soon."

"See you soon."

With that, Ada made her way to the train. She glanced back at intervals to see if Mary had left, but she was still standing in the same spot, waving at her. Ada stepped onto the train and waved Mary one last goodbye before she turned around and disappeared into the carriage.

It took her a short while to find a seat but she did and put her bags down. Ada leaned on the window and stared into space. Strangely, her palms were sweating more than usual and her heart was beating faster than it normally did. She couldn't even think straight. The night before, she had barely slept as she stayed up all night practicing what she was going to say to her prospective employer. Her nerves were all over the place and the train ride had not even begun.

There was not a lot to pack from her former home. She only had two bags with her. A small one, and a big one. When she was done packing the night before, she stood and examined the load she was traveling with. It was then that she realized that she and Jane practically shared almost everything. Whatever she didn't have, Jane had provided. There were only a few things that she had to her name. Jane had been right to worry about what Ada's life was going to be without her.

Her nerves were somewhat soothed when Mr. Peyton talked about his time in Minnesota when he was a young man. He claimed he lived in a nice peaceful town where everybody knew everybody. There were no crimes, and the cost of living was affordable. Although he couldn't recall the town he lived in, Ada decided to generalize and imagine that Fairview was the one. She hoped for a place with no crime, and hopefully, people like Paul didn't live there.

Ada hoped for the same experience she had when she started working with Jane. Not only was Jane nice to her, but the neighbors were also the friendliest people she had ever met. Most of the people in the area were old and they either lived alone, with only their help, or with their children. It was a peaceful neighborhood. One Ada wasn't going to forget in a hurry.

The day soon became night and Ada could see the stars clearly through the train window. A smile slowly formed on her lips when she noticed that stargazing was starting to feel good again. It was a sign that leaving Virginia was the right decision for her. The new breath of fresh air she was going to get when she arrived in Minnesota was going to be different... better.

"Oh, Jane. I hope you're up there and that you're happy," Ada whispered, gazing at the sky. Her eyes filled with tears. "I'm on my way to another town, far from our home. Far from where we have fond memories together. Remember the time I fell from the stairs when I was trying to stack books in the attic? You helped clean my wound that day and you worried all night for me. Or the time we stayed up all night knitting blankets? You were telling me the stories your father told you when you were a girl. Or your sixtieth birthday. We had so much fun that day. Five years isn't a long time to a lot of people, but to me, it was a lifetime. Working for you was the best thing that ever happened to me. I will never forget you, Jane. I'll miss you too. Sleep well."

As she drifted off to sleep she was hopeful for her future, it had to be better than what she had left behind, didn't it?

CHAPTER SIX

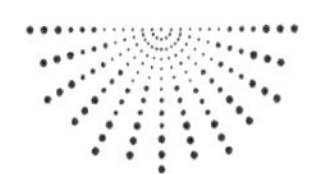

After many hours and days of the brutal journey, Ada thought they were traveling to the end of the Earth, but finally, the train came to a halt in what had to be Minnesota. Ada's back hurt from sitting for too long and she was sure that if she stood up too fast, her knees were going to crack loudly. Mary had told her how long the trip was going to take, and Ada had prepared her mind for it, but it was worse than she had expected it to be. It felt like an eternity. But she was glad she had arrived.

With her heart in her throat, Ada stepped off the train and stood on the platform. The sound of voices filled the air. People were running into each other's arms, laughing, swinging themselves, crying... so much was happening so fast.

Ada, on the other hand, was still processing that she was in another state. That she was away from where she called home, that this was her new life.

It was time to find Flynn Holt, the owner of the restaurant. Ada hoped he had arrived because she had made no plans on how to get to the boarding house. Since Flynn had said he would be there, waiting for her to arrive, she trusted that he would keep his word and yet now she was afraid. What if she had been conned? She had heard some awful stories about people who trusted and made a big mistake.

Pushing those thoughts away she stared into the crowd and reality struck her. There were a lot of people on and around the platform. How was she going to recognize Mr. Holt? And how was he going to recognize her?

Beyond the platform, there was just open land behind the houses. There were roads leading in different directions, but Ada had no idea which way to go. Panic was starting to rise up her chest. People were starting to leave.

"Ada Wright?"

Ada gasped and her eyes darted in the direction of the voice calling out her name. She stood still and stared at the tall, well-built man with dark blond hair and emerald green eyes. He smiled at her, holding his hat to his chest.

"The auburn hair and blue eyes gave you away," he said and stretched forth his hand. "I'm Flynn Holt. It's very nice to meet you."

His smile caused all the nervousness she felt to dissipate. Ada returned his smile and squeezed his hand gently. They had described themselves to each other through letters so it would be easy for them to recognize each other. But Ada had forgotten all of that the second she stepped into unfamiliar territory. "I'm Ada. Ada Wright. But you already knew that."

"Yes, I do." He chuckled, still holding on to her hand.

"Can I just say that I am so glad you found me first," Ada continued. "I was starting to panic and I couldn't concentrate. I was scared I would never find you."

Flynn placed both hands behind him and kept a small distance between them. "That's understandable. You've just arrived in a place you don't know. It's typical to be confused at first. But you have no need to be scared because even if you didn't find me, I would have found you."

Ada wanted to say something in response. Anything. But she was too distracted by the man's smile. There was no explanation as to why she felt this comfortable at that moment, but she did. She felt safe with this man, despite just meeting him.

"Come now," Flynn said. He reached for her arm and placed his hand on it. "I'll take you to the wagon."

Ada jerked when his palm touched her skin and tingles ran down her spine. It was unintentional, and she had no idea why she did it, but Flynn sensed that he was the cause. So, he took his hand away and gestured instead.

"I'm sorry," Flynn said and picked up her bags. "I reached for you instinctively."

"No, it's nothing to apologize for. Your palm was cold, that's all," Ada lied. "I can carry the bags, Mr. Holt."

"Please," Flynn answered. "Let me. It would be uncomfortable for me if you carried the bags. And please, call me Flynn. I imagine we will be working together for a while and I'd like to establish an acquaintance between us. I informed you that I own a boarding house too, didn't I?"

"Yes, you did."

"Well, the restaurant is in the boarding house. On the ground floor," Flynn explained. "That's where we're headed to discuss our business arrangement."

Business...

Ada had quickly forgotten that she was there for a job. She had barely said anything she practiced on the train. The only thing she managed to do was make Flynn feel uncomfortable by pulling away from his touch.

Focus, Ada...

"Thank you for the opportunity, Mr. Holt. I will make sure to impress you. I've been cooking all my life. Like I said in my first letter, I was employed as a cook in Virginia, and my employer, Jane Gilbert was very good to me and we got along quite well. I'm certain that if you allow me to impress you, I will try my best, Mr. Holt."

Ada exhaled quietly and smiled to herself. She nailed it. Just like she rehearsed it.

"Flynn. Not Mr. Holt," he said after a moment of silence.

Ada gasped and turned to look at him. "I'm sorry. I forgot. Not that I forget things a lot. I just mean…"

Ada inhaled sharply and clenched her jaw. She didn't nail it.

"Did you practice that on the train?" Flynn asked, chuckling.

"Yes," Ada answered and shut her eyes.

"Oh. I didn't actually expect you to answer honestly," Flynn said, amused. "But it's a good thing. I'm looking for someone who will take this role seriously. Someone skilled. I'm hoping you're that person. But seeing how you practiced an entire speech on the train to impress me, I can already tell you came prepared. I like that."

Ada didn't want to look in Flynn's direction for he would see her cheeks which were flushed crimson. Instead, she nodded.

"Thank you," she muttered.

After he loaded her bags into the wagon, they began their trip into the town. Ada stole glances at Flynn at intervals. She had expected him to look older even though he had stated in the letter that he was thirty years old. Glancing at his profile, she realized he was just as handsome from the side as he was from the front. His defined jaw stood out and his nose was slightly upturned. His long, thick eyelashes were also very evident from the side.

The man was handsome. She had to admit it.

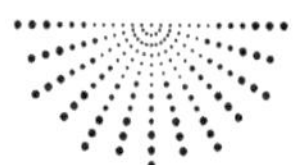

airview wasn't exactly how she had imagined it would be, but it was close. The town was dusty with rough wooden buildings, and the roads were sandy and rough. Ada could tell that the sand quickly turned to mud whenever it rained, but she didn't mind.

They passed by a church, a local market, and a saloon on their way to the boarding house. If she was to judge the people she saw based on their appearance, Ada would guess that they were kind. She hoped most of them were like Flynn. Accommodating and pleasant. It was the start of her new life. Hopefully, if she managed to secure the job... it was the start of a good life.

They sat in silence for most of the trip. Flynn occasionally asked Ada questions about herself and she answered the best she could. Only, each time she would doubt her answers after she had said them. She was trying hard to impress this man but her words were failing her. To make matters worse, she only spoke when Flynn spoke to her and never asked any questions of her own. The closer they got to their destination, the more scared she felt.

"Uh," Ada said nervously. "So, how long have you owned the boarding house?" she finally asked.

Flynn glanced at her. "A few months now. It's my biggest achievement if I'm being honest. I always wanted to own a boarding house and a restaurant and accomplishing that feels very nice."

"Accomplishment..." Ada mumbled to herself. She wondered what it felt like to succeed at something. Ada cleared her throat, preparing to ask Flynn to explain the feeling in detail.

Before she could utter another word, the wagon came to a halt. It was in front of the boarding house, a two-story building with a wide entrance. On the left side, there was another double-sided door, separate from the entrance. The words 'Flynn's' was written on top of it.

Ada smiled to herself, figuring that that was the restaurant she might work in if she was hired for the job.

The walls were painted a bright cream color. It was obviously a new place and it looked welcoming. One side of the building even had flower beds with mature flower stalks and blooming flowers. It brought a smile to her face, for she loved flowers.

"I love flowers," Flynn said. "That's why I planted some colorful ones outside to give the place a feeling of... life, of vibrancy."

"They are beautiful, Flynn," Ada said, impressed.

Flynn smiled back at her and gestured for her to go inside. He walked behind her as they made their way down a narrow passage.

"To your left," Flynn said softly.

Ada obliged and walked into the room to her left. She held her breath when she walked into a small room with two people seated. A man and a woman. The first thought that crossed Ada's mind was of Paul and Clara Gilbert. The couple somehow reminded Ada of them. The lady, with curly brown hair like Clara's, was leaning on the man's shoulder. The man, who Ada figured was the husband was lanky too – probably taller than Paul –

had vibrant red hair slicked back and eyes like Flynn's, except they weren't as deep.

There was one particular difference about this couple though. Unlike Paul and Clara, the duo had beautiful smiles, though Kit had a tooth missing, his smile still warmed her. Ada had no idea why, but she was immediately convinced that their smile was friendly.

"Ada, I would like you to meet Kit and Pearl Logan," Flynn said, standing by her side. "They are the other half of this business. Nothing runs efficiently without them around. Kit, Pearl… Ada Wright.

"Goodness, you're a pretty lady," Pearl said, studying Ada's face. "How was the journey?"

"Fine, thank you," Ada replied, suddenly relaxed. "I sat down for so long, that I don't want to ever sit down again."

Pearl threw her head back in laughter. "Sorry about the stress. I hear you're from Virginia. I moved here from Maine a while ago. It's nice to meet you, Ada."

"The pleasure is all mine," Ada answered.

"It's nice to meet you too," Kit said. "Before my wife here steals you away and bombards you with questions,

I'll take her somewhere else. I wish you luck, and I hope you get the job."

"I wasn't going to bombard her with questions," Pearl argued. "I was just going to ask what part of Virginia she came from. I visited Virginia a couple of times too. Did you go anywhere outside Virginia? Have you been to Maine?"

Kit laughed. "As you can see, Pearl has been looking forward to meeting someone from the East for a while now," Kit said, shaking his head. "Honey, Ada has to talk to Flynn. How about we let her finish her interview and then you can sit down and talk with her?"

Pearl turned to Ada. "Would you sit and talk with me after, Ada? I would love to hear all about your journey."

"She also needs to rest from the long journey, Pearl," Flynn chimed in.

"Goodness, I am so sorry, Ada," Pearl said. "I got a bit too excited. We can talk whenever. Once again, it's nice to meet you. Please don't hesitate to reach out to me if you have any questions."

Ada liked Pearl already. "I will. Thank you so much for the warm welcome."

"Oh, by the way, would you prefer to rest here for a bit before you go to the kitchen, or…"

"Oh, no. I'm ready," Ada said.

It was better to start and get it over with. Flynn had stated in his last letter that she was going to be tested on arrival. So, she had to prepare a meal with whatever ingredients she found in the kitchen. The test didn't bother Ada. She was confident in her cooking. The many compliments she had received from Jane over the years had given Ada a secure sense of confidence. All she hoped was that it was to Flynn's taste.

"All right then. I'll show you to the kitchen."

Ada followed closely behind Flynn. This was it. It was time to prove herself and impress him. She needed to pay all her attention to his instructions so everything was done to his satisfaction. There was absolutely no way she was going back to Virginia after traveling all this way.

Ada had been so focused on her thoughts that she didn't realize Flynn was watching her. He stood with his back against the kitchen counter and crossed his arms.

"I'm ready, Mr. Holt," Ada said, trying to sound confident. "Flynn. Sorry."

"It's all right, you'll get used to it," he said. "So, you have chicken, vegetables, beef... and some other things. It's dinner, so you have all afternoon to prepare whatever you think is good enough to get you the job here."

"Duly noted. I'll do my best," Ada said, feeling energetic.

"Don't stress yourself, Ada," Flynn said softly, holding her gaze. "You traveled for days. You must be tired. I just need to know that you can cook well enough for us to sell it. All right?"

If only Flynn was looking for a wife too...

Ada shook her head to ward off the intrusive thoughts. "Thank you for the concern, Flynn. You're kind."

Flynn chuckled lightly. He reached for her shoulder and patted it. "Thank you."

Ada turned to stare at his strong hand on her shoulder and held her breath. How was she ever going to pay attention if the smallest things that Flynn harmlessly did were affecting her this greatly?

"I'm sorry... again," Flynn said, taking his hand off and folding it into a fist.

"You don't have to apologize."

"And you don't have to call me Mr. Holt but yet you still do."

Ada giggled. "It's a habit I formed back in Virginia when we were still exchanging letters. I used to talk about you with my friend, Mary. We both referred to you as Mr. Holt."

"You were so polite even though I wasn't there?" Flynn asked with raised eyebrows. "You're something, aren't you?"

"That's just who I am, Mr.... sorry, Flynn."

Flynn let out a soft chuckle and Ada got lost for a second, watching his white, pearly teeth. He was even more handsome than she had previously thought. She wondered if he had a bride or was in a relationship, because if he needed one... Ada shook those thoughts away. She had only just met him.

I'm here to work... I'm here to work...

"I'll get right to work, Flynn," Ada said. "Again, thank you for the opportunity."

"You're welcome," Flynn said, walking out of the room. "If you need anything I'll be at the restaurant. You saw it, right? On your way in."

"Yes."

"All right then," Flynn said with a firm nod. "Good luck."

With him gone, Ada could finally focus. No one had ever had that sort of effect on her for a long time. It was weird that a stranger was causing her heart palpitations.

Letting out a breath she looked around the kitchen. "What do we have?" Ada said to herself, rolling up her sleeves.

There was beef and Ada was confident in her pot roast. But pot roast took a while to prepare. She had to give the meat time to soften, or else it would be pointless to even start the dish. Thankfully, Flynn had said it was dinner, so she figured she could give it a go.

She could roast some carrots too and perhaps sear some chicken.

As her plans formed and her confidence grew, Ada quickly got to work. She needed to impress Flynn, but she was beset by a particular confusion. Was she trying hard because she needed the job? Or was she doing this because she was trying to convince Flynn to consider her as more than just a cook?

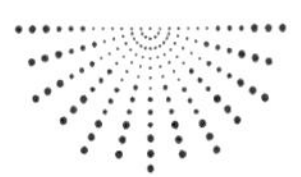

CHAPTER EIGHT

Flynn had been sure of Ada's suitability when he first saw her, but now he wasn't so sure. He ran his fingers through his hair and pushed a chunk of it behind his ear. Did he make her uncomfortable? They had not even started to work together, yet he had managed to make her jump twice.

Even he couldn't understand why he reached for her. It was something about the way she smiled at him. It was like they knew each other, that they were close enough to make contact. How could he forget that he was meeting her for the first time? Why did he reach for her? Twice?

"I like her," Pearl said as she filled a glass with water. "She's pretty, she has a friendly smile, and I can just tell that she's a pure soul. Plus, she's from the east too, so we have a lot to talk about."

Kit nodded at his wife's statement. "If she can cook well, then we hit the jackpot, Flynn. It will mean Pearl's idea worked."

"Can you not smell the aroma coming from the kitchen, dear?" Pearl asked Kit. "I can already tell from what I'm smelling that she is going to be the cook here. I just know she's making a roast and I can't wait to taste it."

"I told her not to stress herself," Flynn mumbled. "A simple chicken soup would have sufficed."

"Oh, come on. You can't blame a girl for trying to impress you," Pearl said. "I know how hard I tried to impress Kit when I first moved here."

Kit laughed and placed a peck on the back of his wife's hand. "I remember how you used to wake up before the sun rose to make breakfast for me. I had to ask you to stop, that I didn't even like to have breakfast or anything to eat in the mornings. Then you laughed about it and admitted that you hated waking up before the sun rose."

"See, Flynn?" Pearl said. "That's just how new brides are."

Flynn lifted his head. "She's not here as a bride. She's here as a cook."

"Well, that's even more reason. Just let her do her thing," Pearl said. "Ada strikes me as the type of lady who likes to cook."

A second later, Ada appeared from the kitchen, carrying a stainless bowl of steaming pot roast. Flynn instinctively rose to his feet and took it from her. Handing it over, she smiled at him and whispered a soft "thank you", before running back into the kitchen to bring the other things she prepared.

A few minutes later, there was a pot roast, seared chicken breast, and roasted carrots on the table.

"Ada, this is..." Flynn couldn't finish the sentence.

"The pot roast took about three hours to cook, but the chicken breast and the carrots were prepared in short order. I hope you like it."

"Well, what are you doing? Taste it," Kit said to Flynn.

"If you don't taste it, I will," Pearl added. "I've been feeding my nose, but it's time to feed my mouth too."

"It smells delicious," Flynn said to Ada. He met her gaze and smiled before turning his attention back to the food.

First, Flynn went for the pot roast. It looked good, was garnished to perfection, and smelled good. The taste, however...

"Oh, the suspense is killing me," Pearl said and dug her fork into the plate. She took a bite and dramatically collapsed on the table.

Flynn felt awake all of a sudden. It was perfect. There was nothing else he could say. He would have preferred to critique the dish, so they could figure out ways to make it better, but there was nothing else to say. There was no word other than perfect to describe it. If it wasn't for his self-control, Flynn would have focused on the pot roast and eaten the whole thing.

"Aren't you going to say something, Flynn?" Kit asked.

Flynn tasted the seared chicken next, and then the carrots. Perhaps he needed to stop pretending and just finish the dish. Pearl was almost halfway done with her portion of pot roast and Flynn wanted some for himself too. Ada made it for him. Not Pearl.

"Pearl, how about you let Flynn get a proper taste," Kit said, taking the fork from Pearl.

"But it's so good," Pearl whined.

"Thank you," Ada beamed, she felt on the verge of leaping in her excitement.

"It's perfect, Ada. Very well done," Flynn finally said. "It's exquisite. I didn't– I didn't expect this."

Ada closed her eyes to stop herself from jumping up and down in excitement, shrieking. "Does it mean I got the job?" she asked.

Flynn nodded and chuckled at the same time, watching the glow of excitement on her face. "It does. Congratulations."

Pearl rose to her feet and hugged Ada tightly. "Welcome to the family," she said.

"Thank you so much for this opportunity. I promise. I will not let you down. I'll do my best. You all have been really kind to me and I really like this place."

Flynn rose to his feet and handed Ada a key. "That's the key to your room. Pearl will take you there. Pearl, she is to rest. Leave her alone. Spend time with your husband instead."

"I know, I know," Pearl mumbled.

Flynn gave Ada one last look before making his way out of the restaurant. Thankfully, that chapter was closed.

Finally, after several months of searching, he had got a cook. A brilliant one at that. Flynn had a good feeling about Ada, and he believed that once the restaurant was up and running, they would have no problem getting customers.

Pearl was right after all. Flynn was glad he posted that advert. Yet something inside of him said he had got more than a cook. What had he let himself in for?

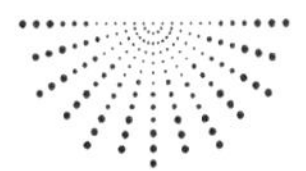

CHAPTER NINE

"I'll be out with your order soon!"

The events of the last two weeks had driven Ada to believe that Jane sent Flynn's restaurant her way. It was almost as if she was back working for Jane again. She felt the exact same happiness, the exact same feeling of excitement to get up in the morning and work.

But work at the restaurant was a little bit different. Here, people were actually visiting the restaurant to eat the food she cooked. Ada received tons of compliments each day, and it was only two weeks since she had started.

Her most ordered dish for the breakfast rush was her scrambled eggs. For lunch and dinner, it was the seared chicken served with mashed potatoes, vegetables, or chicken soup. Ada had formed a routine around her work, hence she knew the exact time to start preparing so she could serve the customers in time.

"Good morning, Ada."

Like she had done for two weeks straight, Ada held her breath at the sound of Flynn's voice. She quickly made sure her hair was tucked neatly underneath her scarf before turning around to face him.

"Good morning, Flynn. Did you sleep well?" she asked.

"I did," Flynn answered.

Ada giggled at the sight of him. It was obvious he had had a good night's sleep. His hair was completely disheveled and his eyes were barely open. Still, he was handsome. Flynn was the only person Ada had seen that looked this good in the morning. It was probably his eyes. They were beautiful on their own.

Instinctively, she reached for his hair and straightened it out. Flynn let her do it each morning. To him, it was probably an innocent gesture, her helping him. But to Ada, it was something more, something she didn't want to define too deeply. Their relationship was strictly professional, he had made that clear. It didn't help that

Flynn treated her really well, and he always asked for her input on everything. There was not one night in the last two weeks, that Ada had gone to bed without thinking of Flynn.

Still distracted by her thoughts, she didn't realize that Flynn was reaching for her too. He touched her cheek, wiping something off it with his fingers. Ada didn't want to jump, so she stood still and let him, just as he always did when she fixed his hair.

"You have... I think, corn flour on your cheek, Ada," he said huskily.

Ada nodded and slowly moved away from his touch. She was starting to breathe heavily and she couldn't let him see that.

"Thank you," Ada said.

"Why do you always do that?" Flynn asked, walking away from her.

"Do what?"

Flynn leaned on the counter and crossed his arms. "Flinch. Jump. Move away when I touch you. Do I make you uncomfortable?"

"What? No, of course not."

"If I do make you uncomfortable, I'd like to know. So we can fix it," Flynn said. "We're business partners. I'd like us to have a conversation where you don't tense up when I get close to you."

Ada scratched the top of her head. Did he really not know why she always tensed up around him? Was he just oblivious of the fact that he had an obvious effect on her?

"Your hand is always cold, that's why," Ada lied. "I promise I'm not uncomfortable."

"Oh," was all Flynn managed to say. "Well, I'll take note of that."

How he believed that lie twice when they were in the middle of summer baffled Ada. However, it benefitted her, but she needed to find another excuse or find a way to stop reacting to Flynn.

"It's a full house this morning," Flynn said. "Do you need anything?"

Ada shook her head. "No, I don't. Thank you for asking. Pearl is serving the guests and there aren't any new customers yet, so I'll just wait."

"We haven't had any complaints so far?"

Ada stopped to think, then shook her head. "None that I recall. There was this one man who kept asking for us to serve breakfast all day. He came on Saturday night asking for scrambled eggs, so I served it to him."

Flynn chuckled. "That's weird."

"He's a customer and they are always right."

Ada watched Flynn laugh and she laughed too. Sometimes, she would convince herself that Flynn liked her more than he let on. There were moments when she caught him staring at her or the times when he would reach for her but stop himself midway because he didn't want to make her uncomfortable. Then again, there were times like this one, when he made it clear that their only relationship was business. Still, that hadn't stopped Ada from imagining a future with Flynn, even though she knew it wasn't right to do so. Even though it was unprofessional.

"Oh, I almost forgot," Ada said. "I made you some pot roast this morning."

Flynn's eyebrows furrowed. "When did you have time to make me pot roast?"

"Oh, I made it first thing in the morning," Ada said. "I just felt like it. I also wanted to have some too, so I made it for the both of us."

Flynn slowly smiled. "Thank you. I really like pot roast."

Ada knew this. She had sensed it from the very first day that she cooked for him and he called her dish 'exquisite'. She didn't make the pot roast for the both of them, or because she was craving it. Ada made it specifically for Flynn. Because he liked it and she wanted to impress him. She always wanted to impress him.

"Ada, come here," Kit said, poking his head through the crack in the door. "Someone is asking for you."

"Who is?" Flynn asked.

"Hiram Collins," Ada answered in Kit's stead.

"How did you know?" Kit asked.

Ada took off her apron and set it on the counter. "He has asked to see me twice about my dish. If he doesn't ask for me, he tells Kit to relay his message to me."

"What message?" Flynn asked.

"That he loves my food." Ada smiled. "Hiram always compliments me."

Hiram Collins. One of the nicest men in the town. He had walked into the restaurant on the first day that they opened and had been visiting every single day since then. Sometimes, Hiram visited twice in one day. He was very smooth with his words and he always had a smile on his face.

Ada followed Kit out into the restaurant and found Hiram seated at the corner of the room with a newspaper in his hand. He had a habit of caressing his slicked-back hair causally before he spoke.

"Good morning, Mr. Collins. How may I assist you today?"

Hiram set the paper down on the table and interlocked his fingers. "How about we try that again, but this time, drop the formalities, Ada."

Ada bit her lower lip. "Good morning, Hiram. How may I be of assistance this morning?"

"Well," Hiram started. "I merely wanted to inform you that as always, your breakfast meal is excellent. I don't know how you get it right every time. You are a great cook, Ada. You should be proud of yourself, at least as proud as I am of you."

"Thank you, Hiram," Ada said. "Your compliments mean a lot to me."

"You're welcome," he said quietly. "Now, I see you cook for half the town every day, but I don't see anyone cooking for you. Or am I wrong?"

Ada smiled. "I cook my own meals too."

"Ah, that's just not good to know. Let me take you out to a proper dinner. You deserve some time to unwind and escape from the kitchen. Don't you think?"

Ada glanced at the kitchen door and turned back to Hiram. No doubt Hiram was nice, and he seemed to be greatly interested in Ada; however, she still wanted to hold on to that string of hope that Flynn liked her more than he was letting on.

"I'm sorry, Hiram. I'm going to have to turn your offer down," Ada said to him. "Thank you again for the compliment, and do have a nice day."

"Think about it," Hiram said as she made to walk away. "You don't need to make any decision at the moment, just think about it first and give me a response later. All right?"

Ada merely nodded before returning back to the kitchen. The crowd for the morning rush was slowly reducing, and soon, it was going to be lunchtime. Ada reached the kitchen and began to prepare the chicken. And as she worked, she let out a heavy sigh. She wondered if love was in her future. And if it was, was it with Hiram? Or was it with Flynn?

CHAPTER TEN

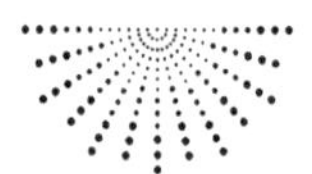

Finally.

The stretch at the end of a long day was always very satisfying. The restaurant had closed and there were no customers left to serve. Pearl had assisted in cleaning up the place, and all that was left was to tidy up the kitchen, and then Ada could finally go to bed. She had done most of the cleaning and only the stove was left. Ada hummed her favorite tune as she picked up a rag and got to wiping down the stove.

Ada had managed to write a letter to Mary back in Virginia telling her all about her experience at the restaurant. About the test that she passed with flying colors, and about Flynn, who turned out to be even more good-looking and kinder than they thought he was. Ada had been anticipating Mary's reply for days now. Hopefully, she was just as excited for Ada as she was. The move to Minnesota turned out well after all.

Since she arrived, Ada had been too busy in the kitchen to actually explore the town. She lived and worked at the boarding house, hence, there was no particular need for her to go out. She had gone on a walk with Pearl before, but they had been talking so much, that Ada had no chance to really see the town.

Flynn and Pearl were the ones that got the ingredients from the mercantile, or whatever it was that Ada needed. Flynn had promised to show her the town when he could, so she could go on her own whenever she wanted to. He had also promised to show her around the area too, but they never really had the chance to since the restaurant was getting busier by the day.

"Aren't you done?" A masculine voice asked, startling her.

Ada turned around to find Flynn standing in the doorway. He was just returning from the supply run, he'd left home early that morning.

"Did something happen?" Ada asked. "You're returning so late."

Flynn walked into the room and placed a bag on the table. "I stopped by a friend's place to talk to him. I got stuck in the conversation and lost track of time."

"Oh." Ada nodded. "I was just thinking. You haven't actually shown me around town like you said you would."

"I'm sorry," Flynn said, massaging the corners of his eyes. "Work at the restaurant has been crazier than I imagined it to be. Hopefully, we have some time on our hands soon so I can show you some places. We're done setting up the place, so we should have some time soon."

Ada smiled to herself and turned back around. She looked forward to spending a day outdoors with Flynn, even if it was just a walk around the town.

"I have some lemon cake for you," Ada said, immediately recalling that she had set some aside for Flynn to get his feedback on it. She walked over to the counter and picked up the plate.

"I made a lemon cake for the first time as a dessert option for the restaurant," Ada explained. "I'd like you to have a taste of it, and tell me what you think."

"Oh, I like the idea already," Flynn said, taking the plate from her. He dug his fork into the dessert and tasted it.

Ada watched his reaction closely. It was the first time she attempted to make lemon cake. During the week, she had overheard a conversation where Kit talked about Flynn's favorite dessert. She had been thinking of adding desserts to the menu option, so when she heard, she instantly decided to make it.

"Do you like it?" Ada asked softly.

Flynn dropped the fork and smiled down at the cake. He was quiet, but from his expression, Ada could tell he liked it. Thinking back, Flynn had never complained about anything she made. He only had compliments for her cooking, and that warmed Ada's heart.

"I tried to…"

"It's perfect," he said, nodding. "It's really good, Ada. I completely love it. I think we can add this to the menu. We were talking about modifying the menu yesterday, so this is a good start. What days do you think we should serve this?"

Ada shrugged her shoulders. "Lemon Cake Sundays?"

Flynn chuckled. "Sundays?"

"Yes?" Ada giggled.

"All right then."

Flynn's smile slowly waned, but his gaze was unyielding. He was doing it again. Staring. Ada clenched her fingers into a fist, trying her best not to look away first. It was as if he wanted to say something, but he was stopping himself instead. Was there something he wasn't telling her?

"Thank you for the cake, Ada. I'll see you tomorrow," Flynn said, hanging his head down as he turned around to exit the kitchen.

Ada didn't know where the confidence came from, or perhaps she had gotten that desperate, but she reached for Flynn and held him by the wrist. He paused, but he didn't turn around.

"Uh, Flynn?"

Flynn turned around and even with the low light in the room, she could feel his intense gaze piercing through her skin. Ada let go of his arm and took in a sharp breath.

"Is there something wrong?" he asked.

"Did you really only send for a cook?" Ada started with a quivering voice. "Or perhaps, were you hoping for something more?"

Flynn took a step forward. "What did you say?" he asked in a low tone.

Ada had her heart in her throat. "I was... you heard what I asked, Flynn. Were you hoping for something more?"

"And if I was?"

Ada took a step back when Flynn took another forward. But she froze when he walked up to her hurriedly and only stopped a few inches away from her face. He had his hands behind him, and his eyes were so intense they seemed to see right through her.

"I make you uncomfortable, don't I?" he asked. "Would it really be a good thing for you if I was hoping for something more?"

"You don't make me uncomfortable, your hands are just... cold," Ada answered, almost in a whisper.

"You really expected me to believe that?"

"You believed it the first time."

"Did I? Do you mind telling me what the problem is now?"

"I like you," Ada blurted out and drew in a shaky breath. "You make me nervous, not uncomfortable. I didn't plan to, but I just do. That's why I'm asking, so I know how to sort out my feelings before they get out of hand."

To her surprise, Flynn lifted his hand to her face and stroked her cheek. Their lips were only inches apart from each other. Ada feared she would jerk nervously, and cause their lips to touch. Her breathing was labored, and it was obvious that she was tense, but she didn't pull away, she didn't want to.

"Is there corn flour on my cheek again?" she whispered.

"Yes," Flynn said, stroking his thumb across her skin. "Ada, listen to me. Right now, our only focus, and the only thing that binds us together, is this restaurant. We make a good team, you and I, and I'd like to keep it that way. I sent for a cook because I needed a cook, not a mail-order bride. If you're not on the same page with me, then perhaps we should reconsider our arrangement. This restaurant means a great deal to me. The last thing I want is for it to fail."

Ada felt her heart sink. "I understand."

"Are you sure you understand?" he asked.

"Yes," she said with a nod. "I won't bother you with this again. I just needed to get the question out of the way, and I just did. You're my employer and I'm the cook. I'll make sure it remains that way. I'm sorry if my question made you uneasy."

"It's all right," Flynn said with a heavy sigh, stepping back. "It's important to clear the air."

"Good night, Flynn," she said, turning away from him.

"Good night, Ada."

His body language was saying one thing, and his lips were saying another. It was almost as if he was indecisive. But Ada couldn't dwell on it. She wasn't getting any younger. With how busy the restaurant was, daydreaming about Flynn and the possibility of him falling for her was going to be torture. She couldn't subject herself to that, not when she had just gotten a job she loved.

It was time to plan the meal for the next day. That was the only thing that demanded her attention at the moment. There could be nothing else with Flynn, despite that Hiram never crossed her mind.

CHAPTER ELEVEN

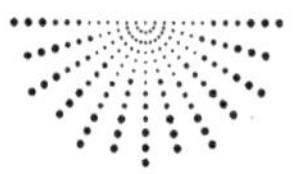

month later...

The restaurant was operating to full capacity. There were more food options on the menu, and new customers came in every day. The restaurant was close to the railway, hence some of their customers were travelers who were coming into town to buy supplies, or traveling through, and they stopped to grab a bite.

Ada hadn't noticed it before, but when she started to see people visit the place with luggage, she could easily guess that they stopped by the restaurant immediately after they got off the train.

If things continued this way, then the business was going to keep blooming. People from the town also came in to eat, the place was always busy.

Ada could now find her way around the town with her eyes closed. She had asked Pearl, instead of Flynn, to show her around the town, and she willingly obliged. Over the past month, Ada and Pearl had become really close. They bonded by talking about the time they spent in the east, and the difference between living there and living in this small town. Pearl didn't have to work in the kitchen with Ada, but she chose to. She was that selfless.

Ada had learned to keep her feelings for Flynn at bay. Thankfully, it never interfered with her work, and she had stopped feeling tense around him ever since he made his intentions, or a lack of them, clear. Apparently, all she needed was confirmation that they were not on the same page for her to focus on her job. She was glad they cleared the air but saddened that he didn't feel the same way she felt for him.

It wasn't meant to be, hence she couldn't force it

Still, Ada was consoled with the fact that they were still on good terms. Flynn didn't let her confession mar their relationship. He still treated her well, and with respect.

He had succeeded in making Ada comfortable around him.

"Ada... Hiram again..." Kit said, poking his head through the crack in the door. "That man is persistent."

"He really is." Ada giggled. "I'll be out in one second. I just need to take the soup down from the stove."

"All right," Kit said and nodded. "But do you like him? Do you like Hiram?"

Ada smiled shyly. "I don't know, Kit."

Over the last month, Hiram had been making an effort to impress Ada by raining endless compliments on her. He had a charming smile that revealed an awesome set of white teeth. It didn't hurt that he always looked good too.

Ada had heard around town that Hiram was a business-man. He made his living buying, selling, and building properties. The mere thought that he was interested in her flattered Ada. He was not shy about letting her know what he wanted. Ada couldn't count the number of times that he had asked her to go out with him. She had always turned him down, stating that she was just too busy with her work. But Ada knew she was still hanging on to that thread. That thin thread between her and Flynn.

But something had changed in the last week. She had started to soften up to Hiram much more. Sometime, earlier in the week, she had seen him in a new light and had been surprised by his almond-shaped eyes, coiffured brown hair, and sturdy build. Hiram was really attractive, but she hadn't seen it until now. Ada was getting drawn to him. He wasn't who she wanted, but if Hiram was serious about a future with her, then Ada didn't mind. She was going to give him a chance.

"Well, one thing I'm sure of is that Hiram knows what he wants, and he has been coming here every day for the last month and a half. He's dedicated. You have to give him that."

"Who is dedicated?"

Flynn walked into the kitchen through the back door, carrying a big bag of sweet potatoes. He grunted as he set them down on the floor and brought his hands to his hips, trying to catch his breath.

"No one," Ada answered.

"It's Hiram," Kit said, smirking. "He likes Ada and he wants to court her."

"Oh," Flynn said, nodding. "That's nice. Hiram is a good man and he's been coming here every day because of you, Ada. At least hear him out."

It was official, the thin thread had finally been cut. Flynn really wasn't interested in her. He had told her this before and made his intentions known, yet she foolishly continued to harbor feelings for him. Perhaps it was time to let go of the idea that she and Flynn had a future together.

Ada sighed. "I'm going to. I like Hiram, but maybe it's because I don't know him well that I'm so skeptical, but it only takes a conversation to be certain, right?"

"It sure does," Kit said. "Go on, he's waiting for you. You both can discuss and set up an evening together. Perhaps tomorrow since it's Saturday."

Ada took off her apron and made her way over to Hiram. She only needed to approach the situation with an open mind. Ada had never courted anyone before, so she had no idea what it was like, or how she could form a close bond with Hiram. But he, on the other hand, seemed confident, so it was probably best to leave it up to him.

"Good morning, Hiram. Let me guess, the food is excellent?" Ada said reaching his table.

Hiram locked his fingers on the table and gave Ada a charming smile. "Good morning, Ada. You look beautiful, as always."

"Don't flatter me, Hiram. I look like a hot mess," Ada said. "I'm pretty sure there are stains on my shirt."

"Still," Hiram said, chuckling. "You look beautiful."

Ada looked away shyly. "Thank you," she managed to say. "And you look nice, as always."

Hiram's gaze softened. He leaned back on his chair and crossed his arms. "That's the first compliment I've received from you since we met."

"It is?"

"It really is," Hiram said. "If you won't have dinner with me, Ada, at least let me take you for a walk or something. I can prove to you that I don't mean you any harm. I just want you and I to get to know each other better. You would agree that I have put in so much effort in trying to get your attention."

Ada lifted her head to face him. "I would like to take a walk with you, Hiram."

"You would?" Hiram asked with a pleased smile on his face. "I wouldn't want to pressure or force you into doing something you don't want to do. I'm all right with waiting until you think you're ready for the next step with me."

Ada shook her head. "I'm ready. I would love to go for a walk with you. Whenever you want. We could have lunch together."

Hiram brushed his hair and clicked his tongue. "I work most of the time during the day, Ada. Lunch isn't enough time to spend with you. That's the reason I always ask you for dinner. I want to be able to talk to you extensively. How about we take that walk after you're done for the day, and then we can have dinner some other time?"

"That sounds perfect," Ada said, blushing. "I'll see you tonight, Hiram."

"I'll be waiting outside for you," Hiram said. "See you tonight, Ada."

Ada nodded and turned around to walk away. Her heart was beating like a war drum. Everything was happening so fast. If Hiram continued that way, they were going to get into a real relationship soon. She was still unsure about the extent to which she liked Hiram, but maybe their walk would put everything in perspective.

CHAPTER TWELVE

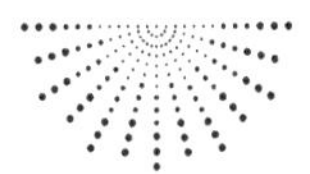

*P*earl Logan sat in the middle of the restaurant, gazing out of the open door. She spent most of her spare time there, mainly because of Ada, her new friend. The sun had already set, all the customers were gone, and the restaurant had been cleaned and tidied for tomorrow. Still, she sat there, staring blankly into space.

Kit had promised to meet her at the restaurant so they'd go home together, but he was running late. Pearl imagined him running towards the restaurant at full speed, anxious that he had kept her waiting. She smiled to herself at the thought of it. Kit was always on time. The idea of him being late for anything made him anxious.

Since Ada arrived at the boarding house and began working as the cook, things had gotten more exciting for Pearl. Usually, she only had Kit to talk to about everything, since she wasn't close to the older women in the town. But with Ada's arrival, Pearl had acquired a new friend.

She recalled how much she longed for a female friend when she had just moved into Fairview, two years ago. Kit went to work during the day, leaving her alone to do nothing. Things got a bit better when she joined them in working at the boarding house, and then Ada came by, and Pearl was content. She had everything she ever wanted. Love, and friendship.

"What are you still doing here, Pearl?" Ada asked, stepping into the restaurant. "Hasn't Kit arrived?"

Pearl shook her head. "He's running late."

A quick look at Ada gave away the fact that she was dressed for an occasion. She had on a dress Pearl had never seen her wear before. It was a pretty flower-patterned, red dress with long sleeves and a square-cut chest. Ada had tied her hair up into a ponytail too. Usually, she liked to tie it lower, by her neck.

"I'm meeting someone," Ada said, reading Pearl's mind. "I'll be back before midnight."

Pearl rose to her feet. "Is it Flynn? I knew it. You know, I sensed the tension between you too from the very first day you arrived. I cannot believe you kept this from me."

"I didn't, it's not." Ada giggled. "It just happened today, it's Hiram, and we haven't had the time to talk all day. We are just taking a walk, so we can talk and get to know each other better. I know he likes me but I'm not sure."

"It's not Flynn?" Pearl looked surprised.

Ada shook her head. "It's not."

"I thought you liked Flynn."

"I do," Ada answered. "I mean, I did... I do... it doesn't matter. Flynn doesn't want anything other than a business relationship with me, and I'm fine with that. It's not like I can force him to court me when he doesn't want to."

"Ada, come on. Sometimes, things like this take time," Pearl tried to explain. "I'm sure if you give it some time, Flynn will..."

"It's really not about time, Pearl," Ada said. "I have to respect Flynn's wishes. Who knows? Maybe he likes someone else."

Pearl tilted her head to the side. "You and I know that's not true," she said.

Ada took a few steps closer to Pearl and leaned against the table. "You know what I want, Pearl? Love. I want what you and Kit have. I want someone to look at me the way Kit looks at you. To care for me the way Kit cares for you. Back in Virginia, I never gave courting much thought. I was happy by Jane's side, and I was content. But now that I'm here in Fairview, I find myself wanting different things. I'm not getting any younger. I'm twenty-five years old and I have never heard the words 'I love you' from the lips of a man. I want that happiness too. If Hiram is willing to give it to me, then I'm willing to give him a chance."

Pearl squinted her eyes. "Hiram? Hiram Collins, the businessman?"

"Yes." Ada nodded. "I have to go. He's right outside."

Pearl grabbed Ada by the arm. "Ada, you need to be cautious with Hiram and careful too. He is not a man to be trusted. I don't like him."

Ada scoffed. "Pearl, Hiram is the nicest customer we have."

"I don't trust him," Pearl repeated. "Ada…"

"At least give him the benefit of a doubt," Ada said, prying her hand away from Pear's grasp. "I'll be back before midnight."

With that Ada rushed out of the restaurant, no longer feeling quite so sure. Was her friend just saying this because she liked Flynn? Or was there something more?

Pearl followed behind her and saw Hiram appear out of the darkness and take Ada's arm.

"Pearl…" she heard someone breathe.

Pearl turned to the side to see Kit with his hands on his knees. He was trying to catch his breath. "I'm so sorry for keeping you waiting. Something came up. We can go now."

Pearl sighed and turned to stare at Ada. She felt uneasy. Very uneasy.

"What is it?" Kit asked her. "You look so worried."

"I met Hiram when I first arrived in Minnesota, Kit," Pearl started. "He was the first person I met when I set foot in this town. I needed directions, so I asked him..."

Pearl shut her eyes as shivers ran down her spine.

"...I shouldn't have asked him."

CHAPTER THIRTEEN

*A*da was nervous. There were tingles all over her body, and the night air felt cold against her skin. They had walked for a bit and had soon arrived at a clearing, bordered by tall trees. It was beautiful. She was already imagining herself laying down on the grass and watching the sky.

"Do you like it here? We can go somewhere else if you want to," Hiram asked, sitting on the grass.

Ada took her seat by his side. "Yes," she answered. "I love it here. It's peaceful, quiet…"

The full moon was out, and its crystal glow lit up the sky and even the town. Ada made a mental note to visit the place on her own time, just to enjoy the view. It had been a while since she had taken time out for herself to stargaze and enjoy the feeling of the night air on her skin.

Ada was still nervous, but she was trying her best to not let it show. Hiram, on the other hand, was calm and collected. He had a smile on his face that never seemed to go away. Ada liked it. Jane always said that people who smiled a lot never really got angry but whenever they did, a disaster always happened. Ada wondered if Hiram was that kind of person. Did he smile this much because he hated to get angry? They weren't close enough for her to bring up such a question, so she decided to wait. If all went well with their evening, they would have several more to come.

"So, where did you learn to cook?" Hiram asked, sliding across from where he sat so he was now sitting beside Ada.

There was only a small gap left between them and it felt a little too forward for her taste.

"My grandmother taught me," Ada answered. "I used to sit in the corner and watch her. We didn't spend a lot of time together. If I remember correctly, I was only with her for a year. From then on I loved it and I just experimented or read books, and asked questions. I just loved to cook"

"Typical. Grandmothers always tend to do that," Hiram said. "Were you and your grandmother close?"

Ada paused to think. "Not exactly. She liked it when I sat quietly in the corner. I guess she was angry that she had to look after me. But that's in the past. I'm over it. How about you?"

Hiram shrugged his shoulders and moved another inch towards her. "I never knew my parents, so I don't have a story like yours, I'm afraid."

"Oh," Ada said, nodding and trying to lean away from him. "How did you become a businessman?"

"Well," Hiram started. "I worked with one and learned the ropes of the business from him. His name was Reed Shaw. Mr. Shaw was eager to teach, and I was eager to learn. He took me in as a child and we became business partners when I became old enough to fend for myself. I owe everything I know today to him."

Ada smiled. "That's so sweet. It's nice to know that you still remember him to this day."

"Oh, he wasn't a good man," Hiram said. "But that's a story for another day. Why did you come to Fairview? Did you initially come as a bride?"

Ada shook her head. "No, I did not. I came for work. Flynn put out an advert for a cook and I wrote back and got the job."

"Oh, that's good," Hiram said, moving still closer to Ada. He was too close now. Their bodies were touching each other. "What work did you do in Virginia before you came here to Fairview?"

Ada cleared her throat awkwardly. "I looked after a lady and cooked for her."

"Looked after?"

"I took care of a lady. I made sure the house was always tidy since I was the housekeeper too. I cooked three meals a day too. I tended to her when she was unwell. I guess I was her helper."

"Helper," Hiram repeated. "You must be kind then."

Ada adjusted her position, putting a gap between them. "So, tell me the things you like to do in your free time, Hiram? What makes you happy?"

"Currently? You," he answered. "You're a really pretty woman, Ada. Exactly my type. Have I told you how charming your eyes are? I could get lost in them for days."

Ada laughed awkwardly. "Oh, Hiram. You and your compliments."

Hiram inched closer to her again and tucked invisible strands of her hair behind her ear. "What do you think of me, Ada? I mean, there has to be a reason you agreed to go out with me today after I've been asking you for weeks. What changed your mind?"

Hiram's touch didn't feel the same as Flynn's. Although Flynn's touch made her nervous, it was of the good kind, the kind that sent soothing tingles down her spine. But Hiram's caused her lower stomach to twist into knots.

"Are you listening, Ada?" he asked softly. "I asked you a question."

"Right, sorry. I think you are a fine man, Hiram. You're kind, and you are a cheerful soul," Ada answered.

At that point, she was ready to leave and she had no idea why she was that nervous. Hiram kept inching closer to her, giving her no space. It was much too forward and his tone was wrong, almost as if he was whispering, and he was looking for any means to touch her.

"I can be very kind," Hiram said. "Tell me, Ada. When was the last time you were in a romantic relationship?"

"You know what I was thinking, Hiram?" Ada said, preparing to stand up. "Maybe we should continue that walk. Sitting here just isn't as pleasant as I thought it was going to be."

As she made to stand up, Hiram placed both hands on her shoulders and shoved her into the grass. She hit the ground hard and the wind was forced from her lungs in a grunt. Before she could think, his lips met hers in an unwanted, fierce kiss.

Fear raced down her spine and she pushed him with all her might. Her attraction for Hiram had quickly turned into utter terror. What was happening?

"Hiram!" she screamed and successfully pushed him off her body. Ada sat up, panting and scooting away from him, but her skirts trapped her legs and it was hard to move. "Why did you do that? What is wrong with you? Why would you touch me?"

Hiram sat up but instead of answering he came closer. Ada tried to scoot away but she wasn't fast enough.

He was on her again and pushed her down to the ground. She moved her head, tried to push him, tried to raise her knee but she couldn't and his lips found hers despite her struggles. This time, his hands traveled down to her knees as he tugged at her dress, trying to get his hand underneath it.

It was then Ada understood the absolute terror of the situation she was in. Hiram was going to defile her.

In an attempt to stand up, Ada headbutted Hiram. He groaned and fell to the ground by her side. That was her opening. Her escape. Without a moment to think, she rose from the ground and ran out of the clearing. But her legs failed her. She was too scared, and fear weakened her knees. Ada fell to the floor, but it didn't stop her from crawling. She crawled as fast as she could.

"Where do you think you're going?"

No sound that Ada had heard in her entire life terrified her the way Hiram's voice did at that moment. It felt like her heart skipped several beats as Hiram towered over her. This time, he was strong enough to throw her on her stomach, and pin her hands to the ground with one of his hands.

"Hiram, why are you doing this to me?" Ada screamed, on the verge of tears. She wiggled, trying to find a way out. "Stop it!"

"Stay still," Hiram grunted. "You're unattached to anyone, so what's the problem? You don't have a fiancé here, and no one is waiting for you. I don't see a problem with having a little taste."

She was pressed against the ground so hard that Ada could barely breathe. All the strength in her body was slowly dissipating as her breath heaved in her chest. But the thought of Hiram taking advantage of her was a nightmare she couldn't live with. She had to fight harder.

Desperately, Ada managed to twist herself sideways and knee Hiram in the groin. He froze in pain and she swiftly pushed him off of her. It was fruitless to try and run with how weak she was, so Ada crawled instead. She managed a few, strides before feeling a hand on her ankle.

"Come back here," Hiram rasped.

He pulled her by the ankle and dragged Ada back toward him. The smirk on his face was more than she could bear and she kicked out at him with all her might.

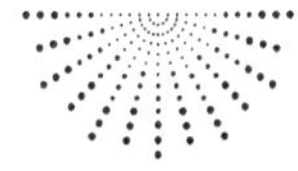

CHAPTER FOURTEEN

"Ada!"

The familiar voice calling out to Ada caused Hiram to pause. Ada couldn't process what was happening, but she had no strength left to fight. She needed help. Fast.

Ada's heart galloped at a scary pace. Her mind was blank, not a thought was in it. Everything echoed, and the only thing she could hear was the sound of her heart beating. Her entire body was shaking. The cold air brushed against her bare skin, dragging her attention to the fact that her knees were exposed. Ada lazily dragged her gown down to cover herself as she remained on the floor, unable to process what she had just gone through.

What happened?

Why?

Where was the Hiram she knew, and who was this man she had been fighting a few seconds ago?

She could see Hiram scurry to his feet as Flynn approached him. Ada could also see Hiram make hand gestures as if he was trying to explain something to Flynn, but Flynn wasn't having any of it. He shoved Hiram hard in the chest, sending him flying to the ground.

"Don't you ever!" Flynn's voice was loud enough for Ada to hear amidst the chaos going on in her mind. She could see the rage in his eyes and his demeanor. Ada couldn't hear much, but it seemed as though Flynn was threatening Hiram.

"I don't ever want to see you anywhere close to Ada or our restaurant ever again," Flynn yelled. "If you try to hurt Ada again, I'll hurt you. That's a promise. I don't make empty promises."

Flynn's voice was steadying her, tethering her to reality again. Her heart was calming. She was still on the ground, facing the sky covered with a carpet of stars. She had a bitter feeling in the pit of her stomach that she was never going to stargaze the same way ever again.

"Are you all right, Ada?" Flynn asked, squatting by her side. "Let me help you to your feet."

"No," Ada said with a trembling voice. "I can stand."

Hiram had left. She had not even realized it. Ada had not fully wrapped her head around what had just happened to her, but she was too embarrassed to be around Flynn.

"Are you all right? Did he hurt you badly?"

"I'm fine," she managed to say, avoiding his gaze. "Thank you for your help. I'll see you at the... at the... uh..."

Tears were starting to well up in her eyes. It was the first time she had opened up the gates of her heart to someone and he had trampled all over her. Was that what he wanted all along? Was that who Hiram truly was. How? It didn't stand to reason.

"Ada," Flynn called her softly. He reached for her and held on to both her elbows to help her stand still.

"No, don't touch me," Ada said. "I'm dirty. My dress is covered in mud and grass."

"It doesn't matter," Flynn said. "Let me see you. Look at me. Are you hurt?"

"Flynn, I don't want you to see me like this," Ada said, visibly shaking. "I don't understand anything. I don't understand what happened. I don't understand what I did wrong."

Flynn gathered Ada in his arms and stroked her back. "You did nothing wrong. That piece of garbage is a good liar. He deceived us all. I'm sorry for not protecting you enough. I won't let it happen again."

Ada sank deeper into his embrace and shut her eyes. "Pearl was right. She tried to warn me, but I just ran off with him. I thought she was exaggerating. I never imagined Hiram was the devil himself."

"He did the same to Pearl too when she first arrived in town and knew no one," Flynn explained to her. "Pearl got lost on her way into town to meet Kit and she met Hiram on the way. She had politely asked him for directions, and he asked her to get on his wagon and said that he'd take her to the address. He took her to a clearing, just like this one instead, and tried to force himself on her. She managed to escape with torn clothes and got help from some friendly farm workers. It appears she was ashamed of the experience, which is why she never told Kit. But then he showed up again, and she knew she had to say something."

Ada shook her head and hugged Flynn tighter. "She saved me. How can a person be so vile? He was like a completely different man, like an animal."

"I'm sorry," he said, stroking Ada's hair. "It's all right now. I'm here."

Ada stayed in his arms for a long time. It felt safe there and she wanted to stay forever. She pulled away when she guessed that she was taking advantage of the situation to embrace Flynn. "We should get going, it's getting late."

With that said, Ada sniffed back her tears and turned around to walk away. She paused, noticing that Flynn hadn't let go of her hand. He gently pulled her back into his embrace and hugged her tightly.

"Flynn, I'll get ideas," Ada whispered.

Flynn pressed his eyebrows against hers and caressed her face with his thumb. Ada could feel his breathing on her skin and in the next second, the tension she had buried deep in her heart for him was revived. It had been more than a month since they had been this close to each other.

"Flynn," Ada said in a hushed tone, breaking the nerve-wracking silence. She placed her hands on his forearms and stared directly at his lips, waiting for him to say something.

"Tell me," Ada continued.

"I don't want you searching for anyone else," Flynn finally spoke. "I don't want you to be with anyone else. I want you to myself. I was hoping for something more."

"Then why did you..."

"I panicked," Flynn answered, already aware of the instance she was going to bring up. "I didn't want to ruin what we already had. I don't know how to do this, Ada. I'm not someone who can talk about my feelings. But I care about you a lot, and I'll protect you. Just stay by my side. I'll try to do right by you."

It felt like a weight had just been lifted off Ada's chest. She had sensed it since the day she arrived in Fairview that she and Flynn shared a connection with each other. It didn't happen with just anyone. It had never happened to Ada before. Being with Flynn felt almost magical. Like it was right.

"You're not pulling away like you used to," Flynn noted, smiling. "That's a good thing. I like having you next to me. Do you want us to go home now?"

Ada pulled away from his embrace and took his hands into hers. "Yes," she said nodding. Was this really the start of something new?

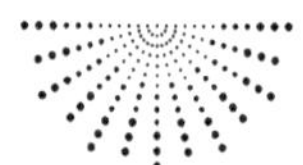

CHAPTER FIFTEEN

"I hope he learned his lesson," Ada said with a sigh. "You shoved him so hard, I think his knees cracked when they hit the floor."

It was that moment right there, that Ada was going to remember whenever she gazed at the stars at night. She and Flynn walked side by side, their fingers interlocked, talking about what happened, and how Flynn had long planned to make his intentions known. It was perfect and it made up for the horrible evening she had spent with Hiram.

"In a perfect world, Hiram would be under lock and key, and away from society. He's a menace, but here in this town, no one cares about morals or what's right, and wrong. I'm fine, knowing that he cannot hurt you or Pearl ever again. I'll make sure of it."

Ada touched her shoulder to Flynn's arm and leaned in on him. "Thinking about it, how do you always show up for me at my darkest moments?"

Flynn squinted his eyes. "How so?"

"Two months ago. I lost my former employer and things got really hard for me. Her son came back for her burial and informed me that since Jane was gone, my services were no longer needed. I had to leave the house. I had nowhere to go, no strength to fight for what Jane wanted me to have, and no place to stay. Then I saw your post in the newspaper and it was perfect for me. I wrote to you and the rest, as they say, is history. If it wasn't for your letter, I don't know where I'd be right now. Then, you saved me again. From the hands of that cruel man. I'm starting to believe that you are Jane's gift to me."

"You're the gift... if I'm being honest," Flynn said. "Do you know the extent to which I am grateful for you, Ada? You singlehandedly managed to bring my restaurant to life. All these people, the travelers who come to our restaurant every day, they come because of you. Some of them confess that Fairview isn't their normal stop, but they always make a detour because of how delicious your meals are. You fulfilled the vision I had for the place and I barely do anything to help you. Sometimes, I wonder where you get your energy from. It puts me to shame. And you always have a smile on your face."

"I wasn't exaggerating when I said I really loved to cook," Ada explained. "I love it as much as you love owning a boarding house and a restaurant. It's not a job to me."

Flynn squeezed Ada's hand. "Thank you," he said, turning to her. "Thank you, Ada."

"You don't have to thank me, Flynn," she said. "Helping you makes me happy. Since I arrived in this town, I've been trying to impress you. You don't know how glad it makes me to hear you speak like this. It makes it all worth it."

As Ada listened to Flynn speak, butterflies danced in her stomach. He knew how to hide his feelings, that much was obvious. He had taken her hand into his, and Ada wasn't planning on letting go of him. She was going to make it her duty to bring him out of his shell. Ada could imagine spending the rest of her life with Flynn. She was excited just by the thought of it.

"You've mentioned your former employer before, and how her son was bad to you," Flynn said, changing the subject. "What did he do? I know you don't like to talk about it, but I reckon you already talked about it with Pearl, so can you tell me too?"

Ada exhaled loudly and stared at the sky. "Paul and Clara Gilbert," she started. "Paul is Jane's only son, but during the time I spent looking after her, he never visited. For five years. Not one Christmas, or Thanksgiving... not once. I understood this because, obviously, people have lives. They are busy, and you can't expect them to drop whatever they're doing to visit."

"His own mother?" Flynn asked. "That can't be right."

"Why I felt angry was because of the fact that he didn't think to even write a letter, even though we wrote to him. Jane at first, then as she became weaker, I wrote hoping he would come to see her before the end. For five years, nothing. But then, I tried to justify it. Perhaps we had the wrong address, perhaps he moved away..."

"And he didn't think to send a letter home on his own accord?" Flynn asked. "There are no excuses, Ada."

"I found out he was actually getting the letters when I sent the last one which was informing him that his mother had passed away. He arrived less than a week later, and he didn't shed one tear. Jane was never cruel to him; in fact, I think her sin was that she spoiled him. She gave him everything he ever wanted. She bought the house he was living in in Ohio, helped him with his business, and paid for his marriage. She did it all. But to him, she was trivial. I could never understand it."

"Why did he chase you away? Let me guess, he wanted to sell the house?"

Ada nodded. "Jane gave me that house, and some money too. She always claimed she wasn't paying me my entire wage because she was keeping some away and saving it, but I know that wasn't true. She was paying me enough, but she still wanted to leave some of her properties and estate to me. Paul heard the rumors in the area and he wanted me gone as soon as possible."

"You didn't want to fight him, did you?" Flynn asked. "In honor of Jane's memory?"

Ada smiled at him. "He's still her son no matter how cruel he is."

"And his wife? Is she as cruel as he is?"

Ada paused to think. "I'm not quite sure. She never speaks. It's almost as if she feeds off Paul's mood. She mirrors him. But my guess is, she is just as cruel as Paul."

Flynn sighed. "Now, I miss my own mother," he said. "She was an angel. She was like you in a way. Always smiling, never complained, always said what she was feeling. I remember the day she passed away. She had overworked herself."

"I'm so sorry," Ada said to him softly.

"What about you? What about your mother?"

Ada dropped her head. "She passed away too. I never really got to see her, or attend her funeral."

"Why is that?"

"Well, my father passed away first when I was about twelve years old. Then, when I turned fifteen, my mother got remarried, and of course, her new husband didn't want any... baggage."

"She left you?"

"In a way," Ada said. "At first, I lived with my grand-mother, who taught me how to cook, but then she passed away too, so I started living alone. I've been alone since I was sixteen."

"I'm so sorry," Flynn said. "It must have been tough."

"It was, but it all got better when I met Jane. I'm thankful for my journey. If it didn't happen the way it did, I would have never met you."

Flynn smiled and stopped in his tracks. He turned to Ada, holding her gaze in a powerful, dreamy lock before pulling her into his arms. Ada clung tight to him, loving the feel of his soft touch and his effusive warmth. He rocked gently, from side to side, and Ada felt even more relaxed. Ada inhaled deeply and exhaled slowly, as she wrapped her head around the fact that she was going to be in Flynn's arms for as long as she wanted.

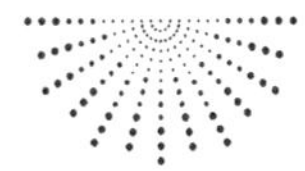

CHAPTER SIXTEEN

*D*ays later...

"I reckon I've never seen Flynn this happy."

"You're just saying that because you want me to blush, Pearl," Ada said.

"I'm serious. Knowing how Flynn is, this is the happiest I've seen him. Like yesterday, I walked into his office in search of Kit and I heard Flynn humming a tune. I thought my ears were defective."

Ada had written to Mary the day before. She just had to. Mary needed to know that her life was as perfect as it could be. She was working a job she loved, she was in love and she was loved by a man. A handsome man!

Back when Ada still worked for Jane, she would spend her free time talking to Mary about men and their preferences. Mary always claimed she wanted an older man because he would treat her better than a young man would. Ada never really had a preference. She never knew what she wanted. Relationships were something she didn't give much thought to. She could care less if they were short, tall, lanky, chubby... as long they cherished her, she was fine.

She had now discovered that Flynn was her preference. Ada couldn't explain the features that made him the perfect man for her, so she concluded that it was just the whole package. It was just because he was Flynn. Every single day that passed, Ada would tell herself that she couldn't love Flynn any more than she loved him. But with each passing day, she surprised herself. Her love for him increased by the day.

"What was Flynn like?" Ada asked. "What's different about him?"

Pearl put the knife down on the kitchen counter and placed her chin in her hand. "Let's see... he would always whine when Kit and I shared a kiss in front of him. He'd ask us to get a room and stop embarrassing ourselves. There was a time he told me that love was exaggerated. He said he couldn't let someone else be the source of his happiness. Flynn always kept to himself. He kept his feelings to himself and he didn't speak if it wasn't necessary. It looks like I'm describing a different person, doesn't it?"

Ada giggled and nodded. "He talks to me a lot. Last night, we sat outside the boarding house and we spoke until I started dozing off."

"Just last night?" Pearl raised her eyebrows. "This morning, he was following you around the kitchen while you cooked; meanwhile, he had work to do with Kit."

"He said he wanted to observe me cooking," Ada said. "He's the boss, I couldn't say no to him."

Pearl shook her head. "You are both hopelessly in love."

"Look who's talking," Ada replied.

They were preparing dinner for the four of them. Flynn had asked that the restaurant be closed after lunch because he wanted to have dinner with his family. Ada had decided to make pot roast because it was Flynn's and Pearl's favorite. They rarely ate together because of the busy nature of the restaurant, so it was thoughtful of Flynn to suggest the idea.

Evening came sooner than Ada had imagined and it was already time for dinner. Ada made sure to serve dinner first, confirm that everything was set before going to her room to freshen up and return to the table. Ada sat by Flynn's side. Kit sat on Flynn's left, while Pearl sat beside him.

"You know this is strange, right?" Kit asked when they had started to eat.

Flynn chuckled with his mouth full. He instinctively reached for Ada's hand underneath the table and held on to it. "I know what you're about to say, Kit. But you don't have to say it."

"No, I think I want to say it." Kit cleared his throat. "We have known each other for over twenty years, Flynn. You've known Pearl for a little over two years. Not once have you asked us to have dinner with you formally. When we invite you to come to eat with us, you only come when we give you no choice."

"That's irrelevant right now," Flynn said. "Let's just eat, all right?"

"That's not the only thing that's strange," Pearl noted. "Look at Flynn."

"I was just thinking that," Ada chimed in. "You look different Flynn."

He was all dressed up. Flynn never cared much for his hair, but he had taken some time to comb it neatly. He wore a nice, white plaid shirt, and a pair of black trousers. He went as far as wearing boots. Ada had never seen him dressed up so formally.

"Goodness gracious," Flynn groaned, setting his spoon down. "I was going to wait until after dinner, but you all really won't let me eat, will you?"

"Wait for what?" Pearl asked.

Flynn pushed his chair out and rose to his feet. Although the room was already silent, Flynn clinked his glass to garner their attention. "I have something to say…"

"Oh, I know where this is going," Pearl whispered and leaned into the arms of her husband.

Ada, on the other hand, wasn't sure exactly, but she knew it had something to do with either her or the business. She leaned on the table and paid apt attention.

"First and foremost, I'd like to thank everyone for coming out tonight even if it was short notice. It means a lot to me."

Kit snorted and quickly covered his mouth. "I'm sorry. I'm not used to Flynn being like this."

"Thank you," Flynn said, giving Kit a warning stare. "I can't stress how great the importance of this night is to me. It's something I never thought that I was capable of doing. It took a lot of courage for me to do this, and so, here it goes..."

Flynn swallowed. "Ada Wright. I love you. I have loved you since the first day I saw you. It was love at first sight and that has never happened to me before. At first, it left me confused and asking myself questions. What is the effect this woman has on me? Why do I feel so comfortable around her? Why do I always want to be in her company all the time? Why do I dream of holding her hand?"

"Oh, my goodness," Kit groaned. "What have you done to Flynn, Ada?"

Ada's eyes grew hot and heavy. Tears were filling them. The dinner was about her. Flynn was confessing his love to her. It was an incredibly happy moment, yet she wanted to cry so badly.

"As I was saying before I was rudely interrupted by this uncultured man," Flynn continued jokingly. "I don't know how to do this, Ada."

"Clearly," Kit interrupted again.

"Would you shut up, Kit?" Flynn and Pearl chorused.

"Sorry," Kit whispered. "I just think you should have sought my expertise first."

Flynn rolled his eyes and proceeded. "Ada, I love you. I'm not the best with words, but I will try to prove it to you every day of our lives. Thank you for picking up that newspaper, thank you for writing back to me, and thank you for coming into my life."

"Thank you too," Ada said, almost in a whisper.

"Ada...," Flynn took a small, black box out of his pocket and got down on one knee. Instinctively, Ada rose to her feet. She gasped and covered her mouth with her hands.

"Would you please make me the happiest man in the world and marry me? If you're happy, I'm happy, hence I promise that your happiness would be my goal for as long as I shall live. Please say yes."

Ada wanted to leap in excitement but she stopped herself. She still couldn't believe all of this was happening to her.

"Well, what do you think she's going to say?" Pearl asked.

"Yes, one hundred times yes. I love you too and I can't wait to marry you."

$\mathcal{A}$da could still hear the wedding bells ringing but it was all in her head. It was a happy day, why was she still so nervous?

There were no clouds in the sky, and the absence of it gave way for the scorching sun to cast its harsh rays on Fairview. Ada missed the rain. She really wished it was winter. At least she wouldn't be sweating so much.

Still, it was a beautiful afternoon. Earlier in the day, the wedding bells had rung so hard that Ada could still hear their echoes. Celebration filled the church, but only a few people were gathered there. Flynn had said there was no need for too many people. He only wanted his close friends and a few of Ada's acquaintances from the restaurant.

Ada had said 'I do' to the love of her life and they had tied the knot. Ada was surrounded with so much love that it overwhelmed her.

When people always claimed they felt on top of the world, Ada thought it was a weird exaggeration. But she understood it now. She felt like an angel with wings. Wings that could actually fly. Everything had changed for her and they had only gotten better. There was a certain peace that Ada felt, the one that only came with falling in love with one's soulmate. Flynn completed her. Like the last piece of a puzzle. He had given her confidence, a home, friends, protection... he was a package. Her package.

During the wedding ceremony, they had said their vows, professed their undying love for each other, kissed, and were officially pronounced husband and wife. It was at this moment that the tears started falling, a lot of them. But thanks to her uncontrollable sobbing, Flynn had held her in her favorite place in the entire world. His arms.

They had proceeded to the restaurant for the reception. Pearl had beforehand decorated the place with flowers and had arranged the chairs so they could all sit together. They had invited a band of fiddlers from the next town for the wedding too and they completely set the mood for the party.

Ada leaned on Flynn's shoulder and shut her eyes. She reached for his hand underneath the table and intertwined their fingers together. Everything felt right in the world when her hands were encased in his.

"So, what's our plan for our honeymoon, Mrs. Holt?"

Ada giggled. "I like the sound of that. Mrs. Holt."

"Is that what you want me to call you from now on, Mrs. Holt?" Flynn asked, stroking the back of her hand with his thumb.

Ada paused to think. "I think I like it better when you call me Ada. When we first met, I would always hold my breath when you called my name. It was exciting. Sometimes, I still do it."

Flynn chuckled and shook his head. "You know, I always thought I made you uncomfortable, but here you are, telling me that you stiffened and avoided my gaze because you liked me?"

"It's normal to do that when you like someone," Ada said and shrugged her shoulders.

"No, it's not," Flynn argued. "I liked you, and all I wanted to do was talk to you and always be around you. If anything, seeing you excited me. It didn't make me nervous."

"Well, I think it's different for men," Ada said.

"And how would you know?"

"How do you know your reaction is the normal one?"

Flynn chuckled and shook his head. He leaned in, tilted Ada's face up with his finger, and placed a gentle kiss on her lips. Flynn let his lips hover over Ada's for a brief moment before placing another kiss on her lips again.

"Would you stop that? It's embarrassing. My goodness," Pearl said, clicking her tongue. "Some people..."

Ada rolled her eyes at Pearl and pecked Flynn before pulling away. The rest of the night went on smoothly. It saddened Ada that Mary wasn't there to witness the happiest day of her life. They had promised to be at each other's weddings, but the distance had ruined all their plans. Ada hoped her friend was doing well in Virginia, and that she too had found love.

Ada and Flynn shared a dance together in each other's arms. At the end of the night, she went home with Flynn, not as Ada Wright, but as his wife, Ada Holt.

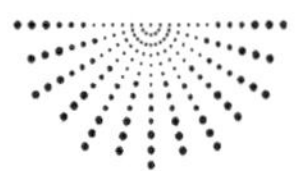

month later...

"Ada, I can do it myself."

"I don't want you doing it."

"Let me do it."

"Flynn, go sit down. You spent all night at the boarding house fixing a roof. You haven't slept well. I can do it."

"I insist."

Ada groaned in frustration. To think they were fighting over who was going to do the dishes. When Flynn had said during his vows that he was going to do everything within his power to make her happy, Ada didn't think he was going to take it to this extent. There was a lot he didn't want her to do. He didn't let her carry heavy things on her own, he monitored her to make sure of it. And now, he wasn't letting her do the dishes.

"Why do you insist?" Ada asked, in the mood for an argument. "I've been doing this in the past and you had no problem with it."

"That's the restaurant. This is our home. Let me ease your stress in any way I can."

They had a place to themselves inside the boarding house on the ground floor. It was where Flynn lived before they got married. It was a two-bedroom apartment, with large windows. Ada had her work cut out for her when she first moved in as a new bride. The place didn't feel like a home, because Flynn was a man and it was simply a place to live. He hadn't seen the need to put any effort into making the place a home. But once Ada moved in, she transformed it into a home. She covered the old sofas with throws, made some curtains, found a wooden table, and brought in fresh flowers every morning for the living room.

The only issue Ada had was that they bickered a lot. About trivial things. While most of their petty arguments were cute, she couldn't help but wonder if it would lead to bigger arguments in the future, or if their relationship would remain the way it was.

"Ada, you just got in from the morning rush. I'm sure you came here to rest. You do the dishes out there, I'll do them here. You don't have to do everything for me."

"But doing things for you makes me happy," Ada responded.

"Likewise, now give me the plate."

"Flynn, I don't think this is normal. We bicker a lot, too much," Ada said.

"Of course, we bicker, we're married," he answered, grabbing the plate from her grasp. "My mother didn't listen to me either and it has stuck with me."

Ada didn't understand his reference at first, but when she recalled how Flynn had said she passed away, she mellowed. He was only worried that she was working too much.

"Flynn," Ada said softly, placing a hand on his back. "I'm not overworking myself."

"Not yet," he said. "But you always want to do every-thing. I understand that you like to do things for me, but you have enough on your plate with the restaurant.

Don't be selfish with the burden and let me take some off of you. We are married now, we should have an agreement on these things. When you're tired, rest. You came in to rest, so do it. If I need anything, you know I'll always come to you. Always."

Ada slumped her shoulders and hugged Flynn from behind. "I'm sorry. I should be glad you're trying to help and I am. I won't do anything to worry you, all right?"

Flynn nodded. "I love you."

"I love you too," Ada said. "By the way, we didn't have that many customers today like we used to. I didn't even make half of the orders I usually do. It was strange. But I guess it can't all be good days."

Flynn wiped his hands on a napkin and turned around. "How many orders did you serve today?"

Ada inhaled sharply and exhaled. "About five?"

"Five?" Flynn asked, surprised. "Just five?"

Ada nodded. "I was surprised too. That's the lowest we have ever had since I started. Before today, the lowest was thirteen and that was the first day."

"That is strange," Flynn noted. "Perhaps it's just a slow day, that's all. I'm sure lunch will be much better. We can't have all good days."

Ada nodded and yawned. "That's true."

Flynn caressed her cheeks and studied her face. "Are you tired?"

"I am," she answered. "I think I should take a nap first before the lunch rush."

"You should. I'll wake you up when it's time," Flynn said to her. "I need to go around the boarding house and check for repairs or damage. I'll be back soon."

A knock on the door got both their attention. "Flynn? You inside?"

"Yes, Kit. Come in," he answered.

One look at Kit's face told Ada that something was wrong. He looked worried and he was panting like he had been running. The sleep immediately cleared from Ada's eyes and she joined the men to sit in the living room.

"What is it, Kit?" Flynn asked. "What's wrong?"

Kit let out a heavy sigh and dropped his head. "There's a railroad strike."

Flynn covered his face with his palm and inhaled. "Do you know how long it will last?"

"I don't," Kit answered. "But it is already affecting the flow of travelers in and out of Minnesota. I don't think we'll be getting traveling customers in for a while."

Ada bit her lower lip. The restaurant depended on traveling customers to survive. It was one of the main reasons for its location. A straight road from the platform, and it was very visible from afar. If travelers didn't visit them, it would cut the number of their customers by more than seventy percent.

"What are we going to do, Flynn?" Ada asked. "Won't the restaurant go under if we don't get enough customers to sustain it?"

Flynn took her hand into his. "We'll remain optimistic, Ada. Nothing is certain yet. Let's just see how things play out."

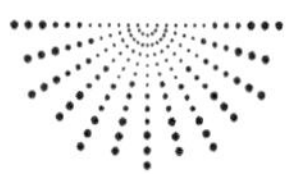

CHAPTER NINETEEN

M *onths later...*

Things did not go well for the next few weeks. Though the locals still came, without travelers to lodge in the boarding house, or eat at the restaurant, Flynn's business suffered a massive blow. The strike ran from July to September, it had ended, but it had ended too late.

To start the business, Flynn took out a loan for the boarding house. The agreement had been to pay the interest in installments every month. Once they were up and running, Flynn had no problem paying back the money he earned every week. He was not to miss three consecutive payments, which he never did. But the deadline to pay back the entire loan was up. Flynn had some money to cover only about half of the debt, not all. Since the boarding house was the collateral he used, he needed to put it up for sale to cover the loan.

The thought of losing it was a disaster. Ada had a headache each time she imagined Flynn selling his home. It would break him. She knew this, and she was sure of it. But they had amassed a substantial amount of debt, not just the loan. There was no other way to pay back than to give the boarding house up.

The first time Ada heard his plan, she had cried. Not only did she love her job there at the boarding house, but it was also her home too. She had gotten so comfortable there. A part of her was starting to think that she was the problem. First, her grandmother passed, leaving her to fend for herself, then Jane passed away too, and then when she finally found happiness again, things had taken another turn for the worse.

Ada stood behind Flynn in the living room and contemplated telling him her thoughts. He was going through a lot, and she couldn't understand how he hadn't broken. The restaurant had been closed now for five days and counting. It was evident that they might never open it again.

"Ada, I know you're behind me," Flynn said. "Come here."

Ada shook off the depressing feeling she had and forced a smile on her face. The least she could do for her husband was to try to bolster his spirit.

Flynn took her hand and pulled her down into his arms. He gazed at her with a faint smile on his face.

"Is something wrong? You've been standing behind me for a while now."

Ada adjusted, so she could lean her head on his shoulder. "I didn't want to bother you."

"You can never be a bother to me," he said. "Besides, I'm in a terrible mood and you always put me in a good mood, so I need you around me all the time."

Ada nodded. "Don't worry, Flynn. This is a minor setback. We can build the business back up again and get more customers."

"Even when we get customers, my love, what do we do about the debt?" he asked in a voice as hapless as his words. "The strike has ended, so more travelers are most definitely going to be coming. But we can't open the restaurant. I need to clear the debt first."

Ada lifted her head. "We will find a way. We have to."

Flynn caressed her cheek. "I'm sure you've already heard that the only way to save us and the only hope for the business is to sell the land."

"That can't be our only option, Flynn," she whispered.

"But it is," Flynn said. "I've been thinking about it and that's all the solution we have. We sell the land, pay off the debt, and use whatever money that's left to try and make a fresh start somewhere else. I could become a farmer. I heard it's one of the few lucrative businesses right now. I used to live somewhere in the middle of the town before I bought the boarding house. It was a small place where my mother and I lived. We could sell it and use the money to probably buy a farm somewhere.

Although he sounded enthusiastic about the idea, Ada knew this wasn't what he wanted, it wasn't coming from the heart. That line of work was never going to make Flynn happy. He was merely trying to compromise for her sake, to figure a way out to fend for her too.

"You can't be a farmer, Flynn. You don't look the part."

Flynn scoffed. "Yes, I do."

Ada shook her head. "Well, whatever we decide, just know that I will be with you every step of the way. We'll figure it out, we mustn't worry. Worrying won't solve a thing."

"Do you want to know the most hurtful part of all this?" Flynn questioned.

"What is it?"

Flynn scoffed again and shook his head. "The only person that can afford to buy the boarding house, is none other than Hiram Collins."

Ada gasped but kept the rest of her emotions in check. It was no use being dramatic about it when they were on the verge of losing everything. Still, Ada didn't want to believe that they had got to that point, but they had.

"We'll figure it out," Flynn said and pulled her into his embrace. "I love you, Ada."

"I love you too, Flynn."

At that point, Ada was desperate. This was a man who had protected her, catered for her, and loved her. She needed to find a way to help him. She'd thought of one way, but it was so farfetched and unlikely that she had quickly shut it down. But now their backs were to the wall and she had no choice. She needed to reach out to the Gilberts.

Ada decided to write to them. To Clara instead of Paul since she was a woman too. She wasn't going to ask for much, or be greedy. But if they had any conscience left in them, they had to know that they cheated her out of the inheritance and the money that Jane had clearly promised to give her.

Maybe, just maybe there was a slim chance of help. Then she remembered their faces and a ball of anguish settled in her stomach. She was foolish, they would never help her.

CHAPTER TWENTY

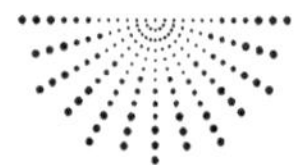

It had gotten to that point. There was no alternative, hence, the restaurant had to be closed down, and sold to pay off the debt Flynn owed. Ada was hurt by the development, but she couldn't even begin to imagine what Flynn was feeling. The boarding house was his dream and the result of his sweat and sleepless nights. Having to sell it, especially to a person so awful, one who didn't realize its value, was disheartening.

It reminded Ada of Paul Gilbert and Jane's house. Jane had grown up in that house. She had memories that she'd cherished forever there too. There were marks still on the wall in the kitchen where she had measured Paul's height over the years. Sometimes, Jane would go to the kitchen to remind herself how tall her son was. There were prized artifacts too, old letters… and a ton of other things Jane left behind. Selling the house not more than a month after his mother died was a cruel thing to do. Ada was positive that he had seen the marks on the wall, and Jane's prized possessions, but he didn't realize their sentimental value. Flynn had to feel the same way, watching his dream taken from him. No one deserved that.

And he was selling to the worst possible person. Hiram Collins. Why did he happen to be the only one who was willing to buy? It was like a slap in the face, having to communicate with him. Ada only hoped that the transaction happened soon, so they could move on.

She sat in the restaurant, waiting for Flynn to join her. They were meeting with Hiram there to finalize the deal and sign the property over to him. Ada didn't want to be the only one seated there when he arrived, so she hoped that Flynn turned up soon.

As if he heard her, Flynn emerged from the corridor, a dejected look on his face. Ada had no idea what to say to him. It had been easier at the beginning to cheer him up, but as the sale materialized into reality, Flynn got sadder by the day. Still, he always had a smile and a hug for her, no matter how depressed he was.

"Ada, I think you shouldn't be here," Flynn said, sitting at the table. "It's Hiram, and you remember what he tried to do to you. I don't want you..."

"I'm staying," Ada said. "What Hiram did to me is behind me. I'm not leaving your side for anything. You and I are in this together, Flynn. Besides, you need someone to keep you in check. I might hate Hiram, but you hate him more. Let's just get through today."

Flynn hesitated before nodding. "All right," he whispered.

Their bags were already packed and ready to go. The plan was to move to Flynn's old house first and set up there, before coming back to clear out their personal belongings in the kitchen and boarding house. Hiram was coming to present the papers for Flynn to sign. Once the papers were signed, the boarding house was his.

"I won't sign today," Flynn said. "I'll probably do it tomorrow. It's a lot to take in."

"It's all right," Ada said softly, placing his head on her chest. "As long as we have each other, we'll spend time finding another path. Where there is a will, there's a way, Flynn. We'll figure this out. I know we will."

Flynn lifted his head to give Ada a weak smile. "I know we will. I might not have a plan yet, but I'll think of something. I always do, and now that I have you to think about too, I'll try even harder. I won't let you down, Ada."

"I know you won't. The road might be tough from here, but we will figure it out."

They hugged, both of them enjoying that tender moment in each other's arms. Ada wasn't scared of anything. It turned out that all she needed was Flynn by her side and she was safe. As long as she had him, she didn't need anything else. She was content.

"Well, well... well. How the tables have turned. Look who came running back to me for help."

Hiram's snigger was igniting feelings Ada didn't even know she had. She feared that if she looked in his direction, she would suddenly garner enough strength to throw a table at him. But instead, she held Flynn's face in her hands and whispered to him.

"Don't let him get to you. We'll be as brief as possible so we can leave."

Flynn nodded and rose to his feet. "Hello, Hiram. I'm sure my agent talked you through all the formalities. Did you bring the papers?"

"Of course."

A slap across the face would easily wipe off the dirty smirk Hiram had on his. And Ada was willing to deliver it. Seeing him again, dressed all smug, reminded her how badly she wanted him to pay for what he did to her and to Pearl. How could a man, who made it his mission to go around forcing himself on women, be allowed to roam the streets freely?

"I must say that this right here, this is one of the happiest days of my life," Hiram said, bringing both hands to his hips. He strutted towards them, throwing his gaze around casually admiring the room's interior. "I never thought the day would come when I would get revenge for you spraining my arm, Flynn."

"Would you like me to break it instead?" Flynn asked, his eyes red with rage. "We are not here for a friendly talk. Give me the papers and leave."

"Oh, no. I can't just leave. I'm buying the place so I have to examine it and ensure that it is indeed in proper condition, one that fits my preferences. When you take the papers, I'd like the keys to the place. I'll have my boys over to check it out and give me feedback on what I'd need to rip out. I'd like to start construction soon, you see. How it looks currently isn't up to my standards."

"Fine," Flynn said, already tired of the conversation. "Hand over the papers. Of course, I won't be signing them today."

"I'll give you two days," Hiram said, chuckling. "But you do know that even if... magically, customers start trooping in, it won't save you. You're in debt. A big one. I feel for you, I really do. This must hurt a lot."

Flynn turned to Ada and took her hand. "Let's go, love." He brushed past Hiram and picked up their bags from the entrance.

"Hello, Ada," Hiram said to her as she walked past him.

Ada felt her skin crawl. "Get away from me, you dirty scumbag."

"You know, Flynn, if you give me one more chance with your bride, I might just allow you to keep the deed to the boarding house. Money technically isn't a problem for me as it might be for you. Plus, I'm that generous, and technically, when I wanted to have Ada, she was unattached to anyone so I did nothing wrong. I offended no one. Would you like to think about my offer, or…"

"Flynn," Ada called, sensing that a fight was going to break out.

Flynn let go of her hand and charged for Hiram. He rammed into him by the waist, sending the man up in the air first, and then into the ground. Ada ran over to him and grabbed Flynn by the arm.

"Let's go," she said to him. "It's not worth it."

Hiram began to chuckle on the ground. "I suppose that's a no to my offer?"

Thankfully, Flynn stopped himself, listening to Ada's calls. With a deep scowl still set on his face, he got back up and walked out of the restaurant. Ada raced after him. Ada glanced back one more time at the place she had thought would be her forever home before getting into the wagon. Flynn needed her now more than ever and she was going to stick by his side no matter what their future was. How could she help him?

CHAPTER TWENTY-ONE

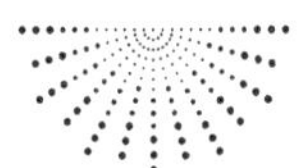

"We will build the business back up again, you'll see. This isn't the end, Flynn."

"Ada." Flynn smiled. "It's all right. I'm all right. I should be asking you how you're doing. This affects you too, not just me."

They had arrived at Flynn's old house with some of their personal belongings. All the furniture was covered in white tarps, the house was very dusty and needed to be aired. So, they started by opening all the windows first to let air and sunlight in. Together, they pulled off the tarps and dusted the living room.

"Tell me, Flynn. What did it feel like when you first bought the property?"

Flynn stopped dusting and stood upright. He placed both hands on his hips and stared into space. "This is how I used to stand outside every morning, admiring the place. I did it so much that Kit and Pearl got sick of me. I was proud, Ada. It wasn't a spontaneous thing. I had dreamed of owning that place since I was nineteen. I worked towards it and I achieved it. Although it was short-lived, I'm glad I got to experience it. But it's not the end of the world now, is it? That's how life works. When one door closes, another opens."

"It happened exactly like that for me," Ada said. "The door in Virginia closed for me, and the one here in Minnesota opened. I'm sure another door will open for us."

"I believe so too," Flynn said. "For now, let's just get our new home ready, and relax. We need a clear mind and a strong body to make any plans for the future. I don't want you going anywhere tomorrow, Ada. We have both been worried sick for the past month. We need to sleep and get our energy back. Once we do, we can start making plans."

"Do you still want to be a farmer?" Ada asked him.

"I don't know." Flynn chuckled. "In fact, I don't know anything right now. I just really want to hold you in my arms. I really want to go back to the boarding house and put Hiram in his place for saying that about you, and I'm trying really hard to restrain myself. That man got on my last nerve."

"Mine too," Ada said. "Still, I must commend you for controlling yourself around him. I know how hard it was for me not to throw something at him. Never in my entire life has a man made me feel the way Hiram does. My skin was crawling, and that only happens to me when I'm around a swarm of insects. I really do want him to pay for what he did. I'm tired of always running from fights instead of standing my ground. Men like Hiram don't get punished, but there has to be a way to bring him to justice."

"We'll figure it out. We have time on our hands now, don't we?"

"Wait, I haven't seen Kit and Pearl all day. Do you think they are still at home? Should we pay them a visit?"

"They aren't at home," Flynn answered. "They are still trying to see if there's something else we can do other than sell the place. I don't think they've found anything yet."

"Pearl and Kit had taken the news of our planned sale just as hard as we did, probably even harder. Pearl had cried, stating that there had to be a way around it other than selling the place. Kit had tried to reason with the debtors to ask for more time but to no avail. They had tried their best to figure a way around the situation, but there was nothing left to do."

Ada was pleased with how she was handling the situation. She obviously hated that Flynn lost the boarding house, but she was all right with merely being by his side. What displeased her was the fact that she couldn't help him. Ada wondered if her presence was truly enough as Flynn had said it was.

Even though Flynn said they would figure it out together, Ada was already thinking about places in the town where she knew people. The best thing she could do to support Flynn was to get a job. At least until they figured out their course of action.

"Flynn?"

A voice, followed by a knock on the door, alerted the both of them of Kit's presence. Slowly, the door creaked open and Kit emerged from behind it. Following him closely, was Pearl. They both looked defeated, their faces sullen masks.

"No luck?" Flynn asked Kit.

Kit shook his head. "No luck. It makes no sense that given your prompt payment of the interest every month, they still refused to give you an extension."

"If they gave everyone extensions, they probably wouldn't have customers," Flynn said. "It's all right. I received the papers from Hiram today. Of course, I didn't sign them yet but...It's as good as a done deal."

"We'll figure something out. I'm sure," Pearl said. "Ada, we stopped at the post office to send a letter, and there was one for you, so we picked it up."

"Oh, it's probably from Mary," Ada said, taking off her gloves.

They chatted amongst themselves while Ada struggled to open the letter. Although it was always fun to hear from Mary, Mary's letter wasn't the one she was expecting. She had hoped that Clara Gilbert would write back to her by now, but that had not been the case.

As she read Mary's letter, Ada's jaw began to slowly drop. It was not the regular letter she got from Mary. She reached again into the envelope and also found another document in it. Ada looked up at her friends who were starting to notice her suddenly trembling hands.

"Ada, what is it?"

Ada exhaled through her mouth. "We need to return to the boarding house. Now. No. First, we need to get to the bank."

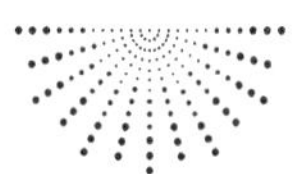

CHAPTER TWENTY-TWO

Once they arrived at the boarding house, they quickly found Hiram in the company of two of his close associates. Ada had not come alone. With her were her husband, Pearl, Kit, and two deputies from the sheriff's station.

Hiram was seated in the restaurant with his legs on the table.

"I can't wait to tear down this place and reinvent it," were the last words Ada heard him say before he noticed her presence.

"Did you come to pack the rest of your things?" Hiram asked. "What is with the posse?"

Smugly, Ada set down a document on the table and crossed her arms. She waited for Hiram to read it, but instead, he stared at her, and then at Flynn.

"What is this?" Hiram asked, refusing to look at the paper. "The only document I want to see is the signed copy of the one I handed to Flynn a few hours ago. If that's not what you're showing me, then I'm not interested. The offer I gave you both when you packed your bags isn't on the table anymore, and I don't respond to begging. So, if that's what you came here to do, I suggest you leave. As you can clearly see, I'm in the middle of a business meeting."

Ada rolled her eyes. "That is a bank note. Not only do Flynn and I have enough money to pay off our debt, if we wish, we can renovate the boarding house too, courtesy of my inheritance."

"Inheritance?" Hiram said, dragging the note from the table.

"It's something you don't need to know about," Ada said. "The conclusion of the matter is, we don't need you, or your filthy money anymore. So please, take your feet off our table and leave."

Hiram passed the note to one of his associates, seeking validation as to whether it was real or not. They nodded at each other and whispered to him. Whatever they told him, Hiram didn't like it.

Furious, Hiram rose to his feet, kicking his chair back in the process. "We had a deal. This place is mine now."

Flynn stepped forward. "Here are your documents, the same way you gave them to me. They're all there if you want to check. As you can see, I didn't sign the contract, and until I sign it, the document is void. So technically, that means you never bought the place."

"I don't care what you both say," Hiram continued with a raised eyebrow. "You think you can intimidate me, or waste my time? I'm Hiram Collins. I get what I want, whenever I want it. Like I said before, this is a done deal. I've spoken with the loan company, and we have liaised and finalized the agreement. It's a done deal."

"The owner didn't sign the paper," Ada said. "It is up to the loan company to come for him since he refused to sell the land. When they come, we'll be ready to pay, with interest."

"How many times do I have to tell you that I do not care?!" Hiram yelled. "Say all you want to, but you will sign these papers, Flynn. This building belongs to me now."

"Mr. Collins, you should cooperate and leave the establishment," one of the deputies told him. "As they have explained to you, this land was never sold and they are not interested in selling it. You should leave peacefully, or you will be forced out of the building."

Hiram scoffed. "Forced?"

"Hiram, the bank note is verified. They have the money to cover the cost of the building and more. We should leave," one of the men beside Hiram said.

"I think you should listen to your partner, Hiram. Get out, now," Ada said with a smirk on her face. "Today might just be one of the best days of my life. Wouldn't you agree?"

The veins in Hiram's throat expanded visibly and started to pulse. He paced, muttering to himself.

"Hiram, let's leave," the other associate said.

"Shut up," Hiram rasped at them. "Shut up, both of you."

Annoyed, the men exchanged glances with each other before picking up their small boxes and walking out of the restaurant. Ada felt pleased, watching Hiram on the verge of a breakdown. She wanted to see his walk of shame. She wanted to see it and commit it to memory.

"Where did you get the money?" Hiram asked, walking towards Ada with bloodshot eyes. "That kind of money doesn't just fall into one's lap. Where did you get the money? Did you borrow it? Just so you can lie and pretend that you can afford this place when in actuality, you cannot?

"Would that make you happy, Hiram?" Ada asked, standing her ground. "Well, that's too bad. Maybe, just maybe, if you got on your knees and begged us, we might let you keep the deed to the boarding house. For now, since I don't see you rolling on the floor, begging us, then get out. You're trespassing on my husband's property."

Ada saw whatever it was that snapped inside Hiram through his eyes. He instantly reached for her and grabbed her by the throat.

"I'll kill you, you worm," he rasped, tackling Ada to the floor with his hands around her neck. "Die. How dare you? How dare you?"

Everyone had their hands around Hiram at that point as he tried to squeeze the life out of Ada's body. Finally, before she passed out from lack of oxygen, the deputy subdued him. Still, Hiram fought them to get to her. He was shaking with fury, a snarl on his face. He truly looked like he wanted to murder her.

"I'll kill you," Hiram kept repeating. "How dare you deceive me? You think you can play me for a fool? This is my property. Mine."

Flynn held Ada in his arms, panting and looking down at her. "Are you all right? Ada, are you all right?"

Ada nodded, trying to catch her breath. "I'm fine. I'm perfect."

"That's good. Excuse me."

Flynn made to charge for Hiram, but Ada held his hands firmly and shook her head.

"It's done, Flynn. We found a way," she whispered. "Don't do anything, I'm fine."

"Hiram Collins, you are under arrest for attacking this good lady, and attempted murder," the deputy said, grabbing hold of the man's wrists. "We brought bracelets with us as we thought this might happen." He passed the heavy cuffs and fastened them onto Hiram's wrists.

Hiram struggled to pry himself away from his grasp. "Do you know who I am? I'm Hiram Collins. You can't arrest me."

"I believe we just did," the other deputy said. "You committed a grave crime in front of two deputies, while you were resisting arrest, you hit me right in the eye. That's an assault on an officer. I hold grudges, Mr. Collins, especially seeing that my eye is swollen. Trust me, you're going away for a long time."

"I wasn't going to kill her, you fools," Hira rasped.

"Don't tell it to us. We just say it as we see it."

Ada, Flynn, Pearl, and Kit watched the deputies cart Hiram away in their wagon. Flynn turned to Ada and pulled her into his arms. "You aggravated him on purpose, didn't you?" he asked.

"I didn't think he was going to try and kill me," Ada answered. "My plan was to get him talking enough that he'd admit to assaulting Pearl and me at the clearing. But it worked out way better."

Flynn shook his head and smiled. "Don't ever do that again, my heart can't take it. I love this place and I would have been hurt without it but you are more important than anything. I would not risk you for this." He spread his arms around to indicate the place. "Understand that. I love you so much. Let's go home, my love."

Ada took his hand and planted a kiss on it. "We are home, my love. We got our home back."

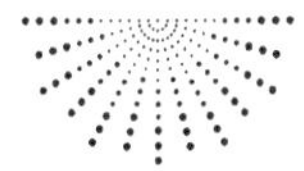

CHAPTER TWENTY-THREE

4*th October 1868.*

My dearest Ada,

I really hope this mail meets you in time. I really do. Tears are streaming down my cheeks as I write to you. I received your letter about how things had taken a turn for the worse for you and your husband, Flynn Holt. It touched me, so I knew I had to take action.

The next day I planned to set out for the Gilbert house, to confront Clara and Paul about what they'd done to you. But to my surprise, I found Clara at my front door, asking for an audience.

Ada, it turns out that Paul Gilbert passed away from a heart attack weeks ago. I had no idea. Clara said he died in the hospital, and she had buried him. But after the burial, she disappeared. I wouldn't say I felt sorry for the man, you know I never really liked him.

With Paul gone, Clara took control of Jane's fortune. She said at first, the fortune was the reason she ran away, but when she returned to the house, guilty for leaving with a poor, dead woman's money, she found your letter.

Clara confessed a year ago, that Jane had written to them asking that her will be rewritten because she wanted to include you in it. But they never wrote back. She still possessed the letter signed by Jane, and she has submitted it to the lawyer.

Now, to the best part. Attached is a document stating that all of Jane Gilbert's money and estate have been transferred to your name. All of it! Clara says she has found a new man, a good man and she is in love. She would like to put everything behind her so she can start afresh with her new husband. I knew that lady never loved Paul. Who would love such a man?

Clara wishes you well, and she feels at peace knowing that she honored her late mother-in-law's wishes.

I also have a sweet suitor too, who is so lovely to me, but I'll tell you all about it in the next letter.

I wish you all the best, my dear friend.

With love,

Mary.

Kit put down the letter and paused to think. "So, Mary is your friend, Clara is Jane's daughter-in-law, Paul is her useless son... and you were the only one that stuck by her for years when she had no one."

They were all seated in the restaurant, having a late dinner. Kit had been left confused by all that had happened, so Ada had to fill him in on the details. Ada was closer to Pearl and of course, Flynn, than she was to Kit. The former knew the entire story, but she never mentioned it to her husband.

The letter she received from Mary, at the very moment when they needed a way out, had changed Ada's life. One way or the other, Jane was still finding ways to look out for her. It was wonderful. Ada owned all of Jane's money and her estate now. It was officially in her name.

"You must have been a really nice person, Ada," Kit said. "This Jane really must have loved you."

"She did," Ada answered. "I loved her too. More than I loved my own birth mother, dare I say."

"So, what arc you going to do with all of that money?" Kit asked.

Ada glanced at Flynn. "We'll use it whenever the boarding house needs it. To keep the business afloat. I'm in Minnesota now, so it's what's important. I will have to keep in touch with Mary, so I can make plans for Jane's home."

"Oh, Flynn is a lucky man," Pearl said. "Your wife only thinks of you."

Flynn responded with only a smile and they all continued to eat. When Pearl and Kit were busy talking to each other, Flynn leaned in towards Ada.

"The money is yours, Ada. You will have things you want to do for yourself later, keep it and use it then. The debt you paid for me is more than enough. I have some money I could use for the renovation and materials. The rest is all yours."

Ada blushed and pecked Flynn on the cheek. "It's ours," she whispered back. "We're going to use it for the business. Our business. It's our business, right?"

"Of course, it is. It's not like the place can run without you."

"Then the money is for the boarding house. Once it starts thriving again, we'll make some more profit. For now, we have money to spare."

Flynn sat back on his chair and held her gaze. "Thank you, Ada. I have no clue what I would have done without you."

After dinner, Pearl and Kit retreated to their home. Flynn and Ada, on the other hand, decided to take a walk. The evening air was nice that day and soothing. Ada leaned on Flynn's shoulder.

"We'll need to move our things again," Flynn said. "It was pointless spending all of that time cleaning that old house."

Ada giggled. "We'll go fetch our things tomorrow. Then we have to go to the mercantile so we can get the restaurant up and running again. The strike has ended, so our customers are going to come flooding back."

Flynn stopped walking and stood in front of Ada. "What's the rush?" he asked, placing light kisses on her lips. "We can take our time. Right now, all I want to do is fall asleep in your arms and wake up late in the afternoon. Can we do that, please?"

Ada wrapped her hands tightly around his waist. "I'd like that. I am so tired, and my throat hurts from almost getting killed by a mad man."

Flynn gently pried her off him and touched her neck. "Do you need to see the physician? I'll send for him tomorrow."

Ada nodded. "It's nothing serious. I must say, I feel a certain kind of pleasure whenever I recall how Hiram was dragged away by the deputies. I'll never forget it. I really hope he goes to prison and remains there."

"Punching a deputy was the icing on the cake we needed."

"The truth is, sometimes it's still difficult to wrap my head around the fact that the Hiram who always complimented my meals is the same one that tried to hurt me. It makes no sense."

"I honestly didn't think he was that kind of person either," Flynn said. "Hopefully, we'll never see him again and if we do, I'll be here, waiting for him. I still haven't forgotten that he tried to strangle you."

"It was worth it in the end." Ada smiled and hugged Flynn.

She made a mental note to send a letter to Mary first thing in the morning. Ada was sure that Mary was anxious, hoping the letter arrived in time.

Ada wasn't sure if she misjudged Clara, or if she changed her ways. Whatever it was, she was glad the woman saved her. It might seem cruel, but Ada was indifferent to Paul's death. It came as a shock, no doubt, but she felt nothing in reaction to it. The wealth and properties he had been fighting so much for were still there on the Earth, and he was no more.

But in a way, Ada was grateful to him. She was grateful to everyone. In one way or the other, good or bad, they all played a part. If Paul had given her the money or the house that Jane wanted in the first place, she might not have come to Minnesota and met Flynn.

Everything worked out for her own good.

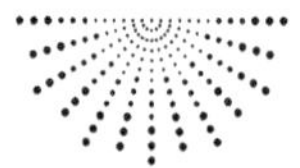

ne year later...

"Ada's Cuisine... I like this name better."

It was summer, again. Winter was officially Ada's favorite season and she was already looking forward to it. Given how much work they had to do at the restaurant, summer was torture. The kitchen was always warm, and the sun only made it even hotter. Thankfully, it was almost over. Fall would come next and after that, good old winter.

"Thank you," Ada said to Pearl. "Flynn chose the name."

"I thought as much," Pearl answered. "You're too humble to have changed the restaurant into your name. You barely even have the time for all of that."

A year had gone by and the restaurant was thriving more than ever. It was now known across the country and people traveled far and wide to dine there. Ada and Flynn had employed three women at the restaurant to wait tables, and a trainee cook, and two more at the boarding house. The boarding house itself rarely had any empty rooms at the end of the night. Flynn had finally achieved the vision he had for the house in the first place. It was filled with travelers from around the country.

Jane was now a fond memory. The summer made Ada miss Jane more than ever. Sometimes, she had dreams that took her back to the good times she spent with her friend. Jane was the biggest influence in her life. Ada randomly thanked the heavens for the day she walked into Jane's house all those years ago and asked for a job.

Now, Jane was in a better place. Ada's only regret was not being able to visit Jane's graveside. She would have preferred to be close to Jane.

To keep her memory alive, Ada had taken up knitting with Pearl whenever they could. They were seated in the office inside the boarding house, knitting sweaters for the winter. If they were going to finish the sweaters before Christmas, they needed to start early given how busy Ada was.

"Where's Betty Lou?" Pearl asked. "Betty Lou!" Pearl called.

"She's with Flynn," Ada answered. "And she can't answer you, Pearl. She's a baby."

"I can't wait for her to start walking, Ada," Pearl said. "I can't wait for her to start calling me mother."

Ada shook her head and continued to knit. They had a baby now, and she was a delight. Pearl and Kit welcomed Elizabeth Louise, soon called Betty Lou, into the world at the beginning of the year. They had not even realized that Pearl was pregnant until she was already a couple of months in. That period really opened Ada's eyes to what pregnancy was actually like. Everyone said that pregnancy and childbirth were beautiful, but from what Ada had seen, it was a mixed bag of pain, pleasure, enforced patience, and joy.

One experience that Ada was never going to forget was the day Pearl's water broke. It had been so chaotic that Ada cried with Pearl. The screaming, the sweating, the agony... it was going to be in Ada's memory forever. The process terrified her, but when they heard Betty Lou's cry, it was all worth it.

Betty Lou was a beauty to behold. She had Kit's red hair and Pearl's brown eyes. Ada still couldn't tell who she took after the most. Some days, she looked like Kit, and other days, Ada could swear she was Pearl's twin.

They all loved the little one. But Flynn had a way with the baby. She fell asleep more easily in his arms than in any of the rest of their hands. There was a certain joy in her heart anytime Ada saw her husband with the little one. Ada touched her belly and smiled. She hoped that soon, she would give Betty Lou a friend, and a sibling.

They had not heard from Hiram Collins in a year. There were rumors that he was still in prison. A year had passed since they almost lost the building to that vile man. Thinking back to that period, Ada couldn't believe that they had been desperate enough to sell to a man that assaulted her and Pearl. If it wasn't for Jane's intervention, Ada could only imagine how her life would be right now.

Owing to the money she received from Jane, their business was the most thriving one in Fairview. Everyone knew them, and almost everyone in the town had visited the restaurant at some point. When she moved to

Fairview, she never imagined herself living this way, known locally and around the country.

"What are you thinking about?" Pearl asked without raising her head.

Ada paused. "How do you know I'm thinking about something?"

"Your eyebrows are furrowed and pulled in at the middle," Pearl answered. "That's the face you have when you're thinking about something. Is it something serious? Something you can tell me about?"

"It's summer," Ada answered. "I'm thinking about the summer of last year. When it all sort of... began. I can't believe how much has changed in such a short time."

"It all started with you," Pearl said. "Everything changed when you arrived, Ada. You put everything in motion. You know, I have to take credit for this. Flynn might own the boarding house and restaurant, but I asked him to write the advert. It was my idea to bring you here."

Ada giggled. "Thank you for convincing him to do that, Pearl. You all changed my life and I will never forget it. I have never been this happy."

"Me too," she answered. "We should go to the kitchen now. It's almost time for dinner."

At the end of the day, Ada stood outside the boarding house, holding Betty Lou in her arms who was fast asleep. The restaurant had closed and it was time to bid Kit and Pearl goodbye. Saying goodbye every night to them was easy. It was saying goodbye to Betty Lou that was difficult.

"Have a good night, Betty Lou," Ada cooed. "I'll see you tomorrow."

"I'm sorry I couldn't help you clean up," Pearl said, yawning. "I'll see you tomorrow. Don't forget, we're going to the mercantile in the morning to buy new pots and some new plates. I'll be here early."

Ada nodded. "I'll be ready. Bring Betty Lou. The last time we went to the mercantile, you left her with Kit."

"Of course, I won't bring her along. Carrying her around is so awkward."

"You're not the one carrying her, and I'm not complaining. So, bring her. The ladies at the mercantile always give us a discount when we have her with us."

Pearl shook her head. "You're merely using my child for discounts."

Ada smiled and handed Betty Lou back to Pearl gently. "Good night, Pearl. Love you."

"Love you too."

Once they were out of her sight, Ada returned to the kitchen to put the plates away and call it a night. Strangely, she had not seen Flynn all day. He and Kit had been busy for the past two weeks. When she asked where they were always going, Flynn always told her they visited the agent and said nothing else. It was something that had to do with the boarding house, hence, she never enquired any further. It didn't stop her from missing him.

"Good evening, Mrs. Holt."

Speaking of the devil...

Ada turned around to find Flynn leaning on the door. She stared longingly at him and smiled. That pleasure she always felt whenever she set her eyes on him had not dipped, much less faded.

"Did you miss me?" Flynn asked.

"I missed Betty Lou," Ada said. "You and Kit took her this morning and didn't let us have her until the evening."

"So, you missed the baby, but you didn't miss me?"

Ada looked away and bit her lower lip. "I might have missed you a little bit."

"Only a little bit?" Flynn asked, casually approaching her.

Ada's cheeks flushed crimson as he got closer to her. "All right, perhaps more than a little bit. Maybe a lot."

Flynn cupped her cheeks with his hands and locked his lips with hers. He moaned tiredly in her mouth before breaking the kiss to give her a hug.

"My feet are killing me," he mumbled.

"Would you like me to give you a massage?"

"Yes, please."

"First, tell me where you've been all day," Ada asked, breaking the hug. "Is it something serious? Something I should be concerned about?"

Flynn shook his head. He wrapped his hands around Ada's waist and planted soft kisses on her neck. "Ada…"

"Tell me."

"You have made me happier than I ever imagined," Flynn said. He pulled away from her and took a step back. "So, I did something."

Somehow, his revelation made her uneasy. He always talked to her about everything before he ventured into it. "What did you do, Flynn?"

Flynn inhaled sharply and sighed. "Remember what happened a year ago? When I had hit rock bottom and I was about to lose everything?"

Ada nodded in response.

"You used your inheritance to bail me out of that deep, dark hole that I had sunk into. You didn't think twice about it."

"What was there to think about, Flynn? We needed saving, and a way to be saved appeared before us."

"Which is why I went and did this." Flynn reached for his back pocket and pulled out a rolled-up paper. "This is the deed for the eatery. A fresh one. I had it altered."

Ada's eyebrows furrowed. "Why?"

"Everything is now in your name, Ada. You own the boarding house, and the restaurant."

Ada sighed. "Flynn, this is unnecessary. You didn't have to spend all this time doing this."

"I really wanted to," he explained. "Everything is in your name, in case anything happens to me. It's your money that saved us, so this felt right. We're one now, and I plan to keep it that way for the rest of our lives. This is my silly gesture of love to you, Ada. You know how much I cherish this boarding house and the restaurant. But the one I will forever love more than all of this is you. Your love conquered everything."

"Oh, Flynn."

Ada threw herself into his arms and hugged him tightly. She tiptoed and planted a kiss on his lips before falling back into his arms.

"I don't know what I did in my past life to deserve you," she mumbled into his shoulders. "The inheritance I received from Jane is ours to spend. Ours to use. I plan to share this good fortune with you every step of the way. We will live together, run the restaurant together, have children together."

"We should probably start working hard for the latter," Flynn said. "I think it's time."

Ada smiled and touched her stomach. "We might need to wait nine months before we start working hard again."

Flynn appeared confused at first, but when he got her point, he gasped and reached for her stomach. "Are you saying..."

Ada nodded. "I haven't told anyone yet. I wanted to tell you first but you've been so busy. I found out two days ago."

Flynn's bright, innocent smile was so pleasing to see. He gathered Ada in his arms and spun her around. "Oh, I'm sorry. I have to be careful with you now. There's two of you."

Ada placed her head on Flynn's chest and shut her eyes. "There's three of us now. You, me, and our unborn baby."

"I hope we have a daughter that looks just like you," Flynn said and planted a kiss on her forehead.

Ada suddenly recalled Jane's last question to her before her demise. What her plan was for the future. She recalled Jane asking her to do something that made her happy because that was all that actually mattered. Ada hoped that Jane was proud of her wherever she was. She had done exactly as she asked and if she had a girl she would call her Jane.

One year down, a lifetime of happiness to go.

If you enjoyed this story join my newsletter for occasional free content and to be the first to know when new books are available.

Read on for a preview of a readers favorite...

THE SECOND CHANCE BRIDE – PREVIEW

(This series of 3 books are some of my favorites. One of my lovely readers asked me if they were still available. They are, and so I would love for you to try them. They are longer than my usual books, which gives me time to get more deeply involved with the characters. You may find the start of this book a little sad, but I promise you, there is a happy ending.

Enjoy this preview or grab the book here)

"Grace, I don't know how you're still standing." Laura Price, one hand still on the harness as she drew the oxen along, gripped Grace Salter's hand briefly. "But you just keep going, do you hear? You just keep putting one foot in front of the other. We'll be there in less than two weeks, so they reckon, and then you can let go. Then you can give in a little."

"You've been so kind to me, Laura. And your ma and pa too. I wouldn't be here now if it weren't for them agreeing to help me along." Grace heard her own voice and wondered why it didn't sound like her own.

Nothing felt real anymore! She had spent the last days wondering when she was going to awaken from the horrible nightmare she was trapped in.

"There's nothing to thank me for. All I'm doing is holding this here harness. I reckon the oxen would just go right on pulling this wagon whether I was here or not. They just follow the ones in front." Laura gave a self-deprecating shrug.

Grace nodded and a small smile crossed her face in thanks. Yet, she could hardly believe that she really was still putting one foot in front of the other. She had never imagined Peter being taken from her so suddenly. After all, what woman of just twenty thinks of such things?

But if she *had* thought about it before, Grace knew that she would never have imagined that she could keep going after such a thing. She could never have imagined anything other than her own body collapsing, ceasing to function so that she could join her beloved husband in the Great Beyond.

And, as she walked along, the sky grey and the threat of rain casting its shadow once again, Grace thought that would surely have been the kindest thing. For Mother Nature to simply let her fade away with grief until she no longer had a need to keep going in this world alone.

To have been spared the dreadful bout of cholera that had gripped Peter so quickly... that had spirited him away from this life within a week, seemed somehow cruel, unfair even.

In the days since Peter had left her, Grace had felt herself turn to anger more than once. The anger was somehow energizing and so much less debilitating than the fear and outright grief. But how could she keep blaming Peter? How could she be angry with him for something that had been out of his control?

He would never have chosen to leave her alone, never. Peter Salter had loved her since they were both just sixteen, and she had loved him for just as long.

Grace's loss came upon her again so suddenly that she bent forward, almost doubled over, as the first chest-tearing sob broke out of her like a caged animal suddenly set free.

"Oh, honey," Laura said, her own voice wavering with emotion. "Let's just stop for a few minutes."

Laura drew the plodding oxen to a standstill and let go of the harness to lay a steadying hand on Grace's back.

Grace was still bent double, her hands on her own waist, as she tried to suck in some much-needed air. When she finally managed to fill her lungs, it was only to empty them again immediately as yet another loud wail of pain flew out of her.

It was a dreadful feeling and the sobs were no more in her control than Peter's life had been. Each sob followed the last with a desperate intensity.

The wagon train had been fanned out for the last few days and it was a relief to be out of the single file line they had been in when Peter had died.

A minister had performed the briefest of services as some of the men, their identities unknown and their faces nothing more than a blur to the shocked and grief-stricken young woman, buried Peter as he did so.

The whole thing had taken no more than a few minutes and the men, adept at digging a grave at the side of the trail, had clearly performed the task more than once as the mighty wagon train made its way from east to west.

But the train had to keep moving and, throughout the entire service, Grace had the awful and inappropriate feeling of holding everybody up. Her world was ending and yet she couldn't escape the sense of urgency, of hurry... of being a burden.

She had to hurry to bury and leave behind the only man she had ever loved, the man she should have spent the rest of her life with.

"There now, you let it all out, Grace." Feeling Laura's hand on her back brought Grace back to the present.

They might not be in single file, but they would still need to get moving soon and keep up with the rest. Grace had a sense, as she had done from the moment they had left Missouri, that the very center of the wagon train was the best place to be.

It had felt like a safe place to her, even before Peter had fallen ill. And she didn't want to end up at the back of the train now either. It seemed even more important to stay in the center now that she was alone in the world.

Even with Laura at her side, still Grace felt alone.

"I'm all right, Laura." Grace straightened up, immediately catching the eye of a middle-aged woman whose wagon was slowly passing alongside her own.

She had never seen the woman before and, given the hundreds and hundreds of souls crossing the Oregon Trail that year, that wasn't anything out of the ordinary.

But it was clear from the woman's expression that she understood what had happened to Grace as she wailed out her pain, her loss so raw and shocking. The woman looked sad and, as if by instinct, looked across to where her own husband was leading their oxen.

It was as if she wanted to check he was still there, not lost to her the way the poor grief-stricken young woman's must be.

She turned back again, her eyes shining, and she smiled sadly at Grace before moving on again.

Grace, despite knowing she should be grateful for the silent kindness, felt as if she could not escape the reality of her loss for a moment.

"I can carry on," Grace said as she rubbed hard at the raw skin around her eyes. "I just needed to have that moment. But I'm all right. We'd better get moving again."

"There's no real need for us to rush along, Grace. Look, my ma and pa are still a way back, see?" Laura pointed back along the trail to where Jed and Mary Price were leading their own wagon along.

"I just want to keep to the middle," Grace said and wondered why on earth it still mattered.

"Come on then." Laura smiled kindly. "Do you want to lead them for a while? It will give you something to focus on?"

"Please. It might just keep my mind occupied for a while." Grace was grateful to Laura and wondered how she would have managed without her.

The two of them had struck up a friendship way back in the camp at Independence, Missouri. Ever since then the two families had stayed within yards of one another along the whole trail. As week followed week, their friendship had grown, and Peter had seemed pleased for it.

Her one fear in leaving their old life back east was that she wouldn't know anybody. Despite the fact she had only her sister left now that their ma had gone, still she had worried about their new life and if it would be lonely.

She could hardly believe now that something so silly had been her only fear.

If only she had feared a catastrophe, a loss of such magnitude it could hardly be comprehended, then she might never have agreed to leave their old home in the first place. And Peter would still be alive.

But finding Laura Price so early on had wiped all her little misgivings away. Laura was, at nineteen, just one year younger than Grace. But Laura hadn't yet found a man she wanted to marry, so when her pa had decided to take her ma to a new life in Oregon, Laura had eagerly agreed to go with them.

As Grace took the harness and started to lead the oxen onward, she felt just a little better. The grief had burst out for a while and it would be enough to cope with the task of moving. She knew, of course, that it was only the very edge of the grief; the seething mass of it was still inside and would, no doubt, be making itself known time and time again.

But until then, Grace would keep putting one foot in front of the other.

* * *

The following day was cold but bright and Grace was relieved by the idea that it might not rain for a while. At times, she could hardly believe that they had set off from Missouri in such fine weather, but that had been months ago now and the season was becoming decidedly wintery.

The guides had assured the weary travelers that they would make it through to Willamette before the worst of the weather took hold. They had made good time and would land early in Oregon.

But Grace knew, as they all did, that there was still a trial ahead of them. There was a single-track pass to make in the mud; the strain of pushing the wagon and pulling at the oxen was a thought most of the exhausted party couldn't even contemplate.

But Grace relished the challenge. The harder the better as far as she was concerned. She wanted the physical hardship to be back upon her so that she could focus on survival and nothing more. She needed it, she knew she did.

"I reckon we'll be heading into the real hard work again soon," Laura said as the two women walked along in companionable silence. "Another mud-filled climb." She shuddered.

"We'll get through it," Grace said quietly. "One way or another."

"We sure will." Laura smiled at her, her pretty blue eyes hiding the trepidation. "And then we'll finally be there. Just a few days and this hateful journey will be at an end."

"I guess," Grace said.

"Oh, I'm sorry. I hope I didn't upset you." Laura's voice was full of concern.

"No, of course not. You never do anything but help me, Laura. I really am fine." Grace knew she didn't sound convincing.

"I should have thought about what I was saying." Laura was determined to apologize. "I should have realized that the journey doesn't really end there for you."

"Maybe not. But at least the traveling will be over. At least I can take stock of everything and think straight enough to make a plan."

"Do you know what you'll do? I mean, have you thought about what you might do first?" Laura spoke with caution.

"First of all, I will need to sell this lot." Grace tipped her head to indicate the wagon.

"All of it?" Laura sounded a little surprised.

"The farming equipment and the oxen will do me no good now. I have no idea how to use any of it and I couldn't think of trying to set up a farm on my own. I'd never make enough to be able to buy the land at the end of the fourteen months as Peter had planned to. He was the farmer, not me."

Peter had known by heart all the provisions of land claims before they had even set off. He had a clear plan in which he was certain he could claim several hundred acres and farm it efficiently enough to have earned the money to buy the land after fourteen months residence, as was the system.

It was going to be hard work, and Grace had fully intended to be at his side throughout; helping him build a house, learning the skills required on a farm. But who was there to teach her now? She would never manage the heavy farming tools alone and even if she could, she had no idea how to use them.

"I have only ever known how to teach," Grace went on sadly. "I have only ever worked in a schoolroom with the little ones, showing them how to read, write, and count. Now's not the time for me to be learning how to farm. Peter could have taught me, and I would have worked as hard as I could, but I have no idea how to do this. I know I have no skill for it, even if I was once so sure I could have learned it. But there's nobody to teach me now and I have to find another way to survive." She paused. "Until next year, at least."

"Next year?" Laura coaxed gently.

"Yes. All I need to do is survive until next year. I'll head on back east with the guides in spring when they go back for the next lot of folks coming from Missouri."

"You're going to go home?" Laura said and the regret in her voice was clear. "I don't blame you at all. After all, your sister is there."

"She sure is," Grace said without enthusiasm.

Grace's sister was a good deal older than she was. She was already married with children of her own before Grace was out of the schoolroom herself. The two had never been close, although they had never been enemies either. And Grace knew her sister would help her no matter what.

Still, the idea of going back east to live with her sister's family hardly filled her with pleasure. But then, nothing did anymore, and it was likely that she would never be happy again. In the end, what did it matter?

"You won't have any trouble selling the oxen, and your wagon is in good condition considering all it's been through." Laura had adopted a practical tone to hide the fact that she was already mourning the loss of the woman she thought would be a friend for life.

"I'll sell it all as soon as we arrive. Everything but my clothes and a couple of books Peter let me put on the wagon." She smiled sadly as she thought of all the little household things she'd put on the wagon only for Peter to smile at her and tell her they needed space for the important things, the equipment and food for the journey.

"I'm so sorry," Laura said so genuinely that Grace felt her own emotion swirling in her chest once more.

"And then I'll find a boarding house somewhere and set about finding myself some work to keep me going."

"What kind of work?"

"Teaching is all I know. I'm sure there must be a need for a teacher somewhere. There must be a schoolroom or two for me to work in," Grace said with more certainty than she felt. "But I guess time will tell."

"No sense in worrying about it before you even get there. Just one day at a time." Laura nodded reassuringly.

"Yes, just one day at a time," Grace replied as she kept her eyes down on the rocky path.

Get The Second Chance Bride FREE with KU or just 0.99 to own

Find out about new releases, get special offers, and receive 3
free books by joining my exclusive newsletter
http://eepurl.com/gP7I6n

If you would like to find all of my books, look on my
Amazon page

While there, click the yellow follow button for updates.

God bless,

Indiana Wake

Indiana Wake was born in Denver, Colorado, where she learned to love the outdoors and horses. At the age of eleven, her parents moved to the United Kingdom to follow her father's career.

It was a strange and foreign new world, and it took a while for her to settle down. Her mom raised horses and Indiana soon learned to ride. She would often escape on horseback imagining she was back in the Wild West. As well as horses, Indiana escaped into fiction and dreamed of all the friends she had left behind.

From an early age, she loved stories. They were always sweet and clean and, more often than not, included horses, cowboys and most importantly of all a happy ever after. As she got older, she would often be found making up her own stories and would tell them to anyone who would listen.

As she grew up, she continued to write, but marriage and a job stole some of her dreams. Then one day she was discussing with a friend at church, how hard it was to get sweet and clean fiction. Though very shy about her writing Indiana agreed to share one of her stories. That friend loved the story and suggested she publish it on kindle. Together they worked really hard, and the rest, as they say, is history.

Indiana has had multiple number one bestsellers and now makes her living from her writing. She believes she was truly blessed to be given this opportunity and thanks each and every one of her readers for making her dream come true.

www.ingramcontent.com/pod-product-compliance
Lightning Source LLC
Chambersburg PA
CBHW061526120726

48001CB00004B/1410